Kate stood staring at her sleeping son,

her mind in turmoil over Parker being taken away by the police. She knew there was more to Parker Buchanan than he let on. But he wasn't a murderer. Why had the police picked today, of all days, to question him?

Her son turned nine years old today. He'd been so excited about the birthday party Parker had thrown at his mansion. A big step for a man who wasn't used to being around other people, especially children.

Even in college, Parker had been the James Dean type—part mystery, part outcast, but always intriguing. Kate had never seen the real man behind the facade.

Until recently. Until her son had won him over.

* * *

REUNION REVELATIONS: Secrets surface when old friends—and foes—get together.

Books by Lenora Worth

Love Inspired Suspense

Fatal Image #38
Secret Agent Minister #68
A Face in the Shadows #100

Love Inspired

The Wedding Quilt #12
Logan's Child #26
*I'll Be Home
   for Christmas* #44
Wedding at Wildwood #53
His Brother's Wife #82
Ben's Bundle of Joy #99
The Reluctant Hero #108
One Golden Christmas #122
†*When Love Came To Town* #142
†*Something Beautiful* #169
†*Lacey's Retreat* #184

Steeple Hill

After the Storm

‡*The Carpenter's Wife* #211
‡*Heart of Stone* #227
‡*A Tender Touch* #269
A Certain Hope #311
A Perfect Love #330
A Leap of Faith #336
Christmas Homecoming #376
Mountain Sanctuary #437

†In the Garden
‡Sunset Island
*Texas Hearts

LENORA WORTH

has written more than thirty books, most of those for Steeple Hill. She also works freelance for a local magazine, where she has written monthly opinion columns, feature articles and social commentaries. She also wrote for five years for the local paper. Married to her high school sweetheart for thirty-two years, Lenora lives in Louisiana and has two grown children and a cat. She loves to read, take long walks and sit in her garden.

A Face in the Shadows

LENORA WORTH

Steeple
Hill®

Published by Steeple Hill Books™

Special thanks and acknowledgment to Lenora Worth for her contribution to the REUNION REVELATIONS miniseries.

STEEPLE HILL BOOKS

Steeple Hill®

ISBN-13: 978-0-373-44290-4
ISBN-10: 0-373-44290-4

A FACE IN THE SHADOWS

Copyright © 2008 by Harlequin Books S.A.

www.SteepleHill.com

Printed in U.S.A.

He reveals the deep things of darkness
and brings deep shadows into the light.
—*Job* 12:22

To Val Hansen, Shirlee McCoy, Margaret Daley, Carol Steward and Marta Perry, my fellow conspirators! I will always remember our time together working on this project!

PROLOGUE

"Mr. Buchanan, you need to come down to the station with us."

Parker Buchanan looked from the two officers standing at the front door of his house to the woman standing in shock behind him. Before he could speak, Kate Brooks pushed her way around him.

"What are you talking about?" she asked, glaring at the investigators, daring either of them to step forward.

Out in the backyard, her son's ninth birthday party was in full swing and Parker didn't want this to ruin Brandon's big day. "What do you want?" he asked, his tone firm and in control in spite of the tremors pushing through his pulse.

"We just need to ask you some questions," one of the officers answered.

Parker knew both of them. He'd gone to college with Nikki Rivers and he'd seen her partner, Jim Anderson, around town. And he knew why they were here. In fact, he'd been expecting this visit for a while now. Ever since the body of a classmate, Josie Skerritt, had been discovered a few months ago buried on the campus grounds, their entire graduating class had become suspects. Then Cassie Winters's brother, Scott, had died mysteriously just a few months ago. Everyone who'd known either Josie or Scott had been questioned. Now, it would seem, Parker's number was up. He glanced at Kate, thinking it made sense that their time together would have to come to an end. Wasn't that just his luck? Whenever something good started happening in his life, the bad was soon to follow.

"Let me get my jacket and cane," Parker said, pulling Kate back away from the door. He limped to a nearby umbrella stand and grabbed one of his many walking sticks. The one he picked up now had a scrolled silver handle. A bit of embellishment to compensate for his permanent disability.

"They can't do this," Kate said, turning toward him, her blue eyes full of doubt and fear. "Parker, you should call Seth, at least. You might need a lawyer."

"I don't have anything to hide," he replied, memories swirling like ink spots in front of his eyes. "Look, Josie knew all of us. It's only natural they'd want to question me again, especially since she and I were good friends." He gave Kate a warning look, then glanced toward the officers. "I'm surprised they haven't already called me. And I do have something that might interest them, remember?"

Kate stood back, her hands at her sides. "But…they want to take you with them—that sounds more like an arrest." She turned toward Nikki. "Can't you just talk to us here? C'mon inside where we can talk privately and I'll make some coffee."

Nikki shook her head then looked down at the planked porch floor. "Sorry, we can't do that, Kate. We've been ordered to bring him in—just for questioning."

"And we can't go into the details," Jim said, his tone apologetic. Then he looked back at Parker. "It shouldn't take too long."

Parker nodded, then tugged on his jacket. "I'll be back soon," he told Kate, hoping that was the truth. "Just stay here and keep the party going. Wait for me, okay?"

Kate gave a quick nod. "I'll be right here, I promise. But what should I tell Brandon?" she asked, her blue eyes widening. "He's going to wonder why you're not out there with everyone?"

Parker leaned close, taking in the floral scent of her perfume. Wrapping his arms around her, he gave her a light hug, then closed his eyes to block out the memories. "Tell him I'm helping the police find the bad guy."

Then he let her go and left with the two officers.

ONE

It had been at the Magnolia Falls College reunion last summer when he'd first seen her again.

She was standing out on the veranda, leaning over the stone banister, looking down on the grounds of Mossy Oak Inn's expansive gardens. Her dress was a shimmering white, sleeveless and flowing, the long skirt petaled out around her like the magnolia blossoms glistening in the trees just beyond the stone terrace. She had her hair pulled up, the light-brown curls cascading around a sparkling jeweled hair clasp.

Parker could almost smell her perfume, even though he stood across the elegant dining room near the staircase.

Should he go and say hi to Kate?

No, he thought, bitterness cloaking him, making him shrink back against the staircase. He looked down at the pearl-handled cane resting in the crook of his arm, the glimmer of the marbled white mother-of-pearl contrasting sharply with the jet black of his tailor-made tuxedo.

No, he couldn't go and speak to Kate. He'd rather stand here longing, remembering how he'd sat behind her in advanced economics class their senior year of college, drawing sketches of her. He'd almost failed that class, simply because he spent most of his time with his eyes closed, enjoying the gardenia scent of Kate's perfume. And when his eyes were open, well, that was a different matter. He'd seen a lot; but no one had seemed to notice him back then. It was as if he'd been invisible. But not to Kate, never to pretty Kathleen Brooks—now Kathleen Sinclair. Kate always had a smile for everyone. Even a nobody like Parker Buchanan.

And now he was rich and famous and everyone noticed him to the point of being intrusive, which was why he'd almost skipped tonight. Except, he wanted to see Kate again. He wanted to see that pretty smile.

He wanted to close his eyes and remember that smile.

A hand on his arm stopped him. "Parker?"

Parker turned to find an elegant blonde grinning at him. "Stephanie?"

Steff Kessler's grin turned into a becoming smile as she brushed back her bobbed hair. "Yes, it's me. Parker, I'm so glad you changed your mind and decided to come tonight. How are you?"

Parker took the hand she offered, glad to see a familiar face even if he and Stephanie Kessler hadn't been very close in college. "I'm okay. A bit nervous, I guess."

Steff nodded, seeming just as awkward as he felt. "Well, so am I, only because I want this night to be perfect. But I guess you're nervous because you might be afraid of too many adoring fans, right? Since you've been back in Magnolia Falls, I've heard only good things about your success." She leaned close and whispered, "In case you don't know this, you have a certain reputation—you're rumored to be a bit of a recluse."

Parker looked at the woman out on the terrace. He

didn't listen to rumors. "Yeah, you could say that. Work keeps me busy."

Steff glanced toward where Parker was looking. "Well, from what I hear, kids love your comic books." She let out a dainty sigh. "What's that like, writing about superheroes all the time?"

Parker tore his gaze away from Kate. "It pays the rent."

"In a big way apparently," she replied, grinning again. "We all thought it was so great when you bought Magnolia Hall."

"I just always liked the house," Parker replied with a shrug, reluctant to discuss his wealth or his personal life. What did it matter? He was still all alone. Telling himself he liked things that way, he turned to face Steff again. "I think I'll go find something to drink."

Steff nodded. "Please do. We have freshly squeezed lemonade and anything else you might want to drink. And get something to eat, too. I don't want all this food to go to waste." Then she glanced around. "And I'd better get back to making sure things are running smoothly. I can't wait to see the old gang again."

"I suppose that's the plan," Parker responded. "After you."

He didn't miss the way Steff glanced at his cane. So he saved her the embarrassment of asking about that. "Three operations and this is the best I can get. A slight limp and a cane on my arm, just in case I fall on my face."

A sympathetic look passed over Steff's face. "I'm sorry you had to go through that. We don't hear much from Penny, even though I often think about how she left, all alone with a little baby. Do you ever talk to her or Josie at all?"

"No, I haven't heard from Josie since we graduated," Parker replied. "And Penny probably still blames me for the car wreck, even though she was the one at fault."

"Well, I'd say you've suffered enough because of that night."

"You think so?" Parker asked, wondering if he'd ever be free of his guilt and his sins. Tonight of all nights, he didn't want to remember the horrible wreck that had changed his life. In some ways, he owed his career to that accident, since he'd spent most of his time in the hospital drawing. But on the other hand, that night had damaged him in more ways than just the physical injury he would always bear. And people wondered why he was a recluse.

Steff gave him a thoughtful look. "Maybe tonight should be about enjoying the good memories and not dwelling on the bad ones," she said, lifting her chin toward the crowd roaming around the Mossy Oak dining room. "After all, we only have to do this once a decade. I hope."

That made Parker smile. "Me, too."

Then he looked back out to the terrace.

And saw Kate Brooks staring across the room at him.

Kate first saw him standing by the staircase, looking as if he'd stepped out of an eighteenth-century novel. The brooding blue-green eyes, the dark-blond hair, the expertly tailored tuxedo. And the cane.

Parker Buchanan probably thought the cane only drew attention to his disability, but to Kate, it made him look debonair and mysterious. Then she had to smile.

Parker *was* debonair and mysterious. Or at least that's

what everyone around Magnolia Falls thought. He'd come back a few years ago, successful and wealthy thanks to the popularity of his Patchman comic-book series and the toys and games that went along with it. That return in itself had been enough to send the gossip mongers over the edge, but when he'd bought Magnolia Hall, the old, falling-down antebellum house that had once belonged to the town's founder, well, that bold step had sent his reputation right into legendary proportions. Parker had painstakingly repaired and remodeled the elegant old house, leaving no detail untouched. It was said that the house had been rebuilt to the exact specifications of the original design and that the furnishings ranged from priceless antiques to quirky modern art.

It was said, but it was hard to know for sure, since Parker rarely allowed anyone into his mansion on the hill. Not even his old college friends. Most of the information had come from the construction crews and interior decorators, but even they didn't talk about it too much. Parker demanded that kind of privacy now.

And while Kate herself had only been back a few months, she couldn't help but think about Parker each time she drove by the columned white mansion. What did one man do all day inside a six-bedroom, six-thousand-square-foot house?

In Parker's case, he worked. Day and night, according to the few people who'd been inside the house since he'd started occupying it.

Had he come home on purpose, to thumb his nose at all the people who'd scorned him in the past? To show those who'd pitied him after the accident that he could still stand tall and hold his head up high?

Kate couldn't stop staring at him. He was certainly holding his head up tonight. He looked as resigned and arrogant as a European aristocrat. And—she realized— he was walking toward her. Her heart seemed to be beating in rhythm with his cane as he made his way across the room. Trying to smile, she started to walk toward him as well, anxious to say hello, anxious to ask him how he was doing these days.

Anxious to get to know the Parker Buchanan who still remained a mystery to her, even after all these years.

Parker sat in the dank, stuffy police station, waiting to be interrogated one more time. How had it all come to this? He'd lived a quiet, law-abiding life since he'd returned to Magnolia Falls. And now, just when his life had taken a turn for the better because of Kate and Brandon, it had also taken a turn for the worse. What if he were arrested for Josie's murder? Who would believe that he was innocent? And how could he ever prove it?

Kate would believe him, he thought, his prayers holding him steady. Kate would have to believe him.

Trying to take his mind off his current circumstances, he thought back over the night of the reunion, and re-membered how Kate had come back into his life for that brief time, her presence brightening his world like a flower opening to full bloom.

Parker couldn't believe Kate was actually coming to meet him. He had to remember to breathe. Just seeing Kate again caused his heart rate to accelerate. Leaning heavily on his cane, he watched her moving gracefully across the room, her smile shy and uncertain.

"Parker," she said as they met in the middle of the dining room, just underneath one of the gleaming chandeliers. "It's so good to see you again."

"You, too," he said, his voice sounding raw and husky. Trying to find his courage, he nodded. "You look great."

She smiled again. "Thanks. I splurged on this dress."

"I'd say it was worth it," he responded, his heart warming to her smile. He might just make it through this yet. "How have you been?"

She shrugged, glanced around. "Oh, I'm doing fine. I'm a nurse now, at Magnolia Medical Center, in the neonatal department."

That threw Parker. "Wow. And here I thought you'd gone off to find fame and fortune in Nashville."

She shook her head, causing her dangling earrings to sway. "Oh, I went to Nashville, all right. But the only things I found were heartache and a…a man who turned out to be the worst husband possible. But one good thing came out of it—we had a beautiful child together. We divorced five years ago, and then I went back to school to become a nurse. I like being able to support myself and Brandon."

"Brandon? You have a son." It was a statement, an acknowledgment to all that he'd missed in life—a family, a real home. Kate had had that. And apparently lost it. "I'm sorry about the divorce. But…your ex-husband must have been a real loser to let you go."

She seemed surprised at that declaration, and a bit embarrassed. "It wasn't all his fault. I wanted a career and I guess I neglected him. Then when Brandon came along, things got better for a while, but by then my career had fizzled out and so had his patience. Apparently even though he resented my career, he had plans to capitalize on it. When his meal ticket ran out, so did he. Brought me down to earth pretty quickly."

Parker let that soak in. "Do you ever sing anymore?"

"Oh, yes, but only at church functions and hospital get-togethers. Around work, they call me the singing nurse. I like to sing lullabies to the tiny babies in neonatal."

Parker could just imagine her standing over a struggling infant, humming some soft sweet tune. He remembered hearing her sing in the college choir. Her solos had always been his favorite parts of those staid, proper concerts.

"I think that's a very noble cause," he said, wondering exactly when he'd forgotten how to speak without sounding like an imbecile. "I'm glad you still sing."

She grinned. "Ah, but singing doesn't pay the bills. I have a son to support now, since his father isn't known for being dependable." She let out a soft sigh. "Brandon is my first priority now."

Before he could stop himself, Parker blurted, "I'd like to meet him sometime."

She laughed. "Oh, Brandon would love that. He has several Patchman toys and he reads your comic books all the time. I find them hidden in his bedcovers, even when he's supposed to go to sleep early. He can't make out all the words since he's only eight, but he sure can memorize the pictures."

"A picture tells a thousand words," Parker replied, thinking her obvious love for her son spoke volumes. "It was nice to see you again, Kate."

"Nice to see you again, too. Wow, I can't wait to tell everyone at work I actually talked to the famous Parker Buchanan."

Her words hit Parker the wrong way. Was she just like everyone else, only wanting to speak to him because he was "somebody" now? He should have known. But…this was Kate. She'd always been polite to everyone. Parker had been away from his college friends for so long, he wasn't sure who he could trust. But he wanted to trust Kate.

"I guess I'd better find a seat," he said, ready to move on. If he didn't expect much, he wouldn't be disappointed.

Kate looked confused and hurt, but nodded. "All right. And Parker, I'd love to get together with you sometime. Now that we're both back here, no reason we can't stay in touch."

"Right," he replied, thinking she was once again just being polite. "I'll make a note of that."

He took his cane and turned to leave, thinking he might just have to skip the fancy meal Steff had planned after all. He suddenly didn't feel like going down memory lane.

But when he turned back to look at Kate, she was still standing there, that puzzled expression on her pretty face. Then she said something that really put his head in a dizzying spin.

"I still have it, you know."

An alarm went off in his head. "Have…what?"

"The sketch you drew of me, remember?"

He'd only drawn her face about a thousand times, so yes, he did remember. "Yeah, sure."

"You always were talented, Parker. I'm glad you kept at it."

"Thanks." He watched as she turned and walked away. And he had to wonder if he'd somehow misread her. Maybe Kate Brooks truly did want to take up where they'd left off, if only for the sake of their old friendship.

A friendship that could have been so much more, if they'd been given a chance.

A tap on Parker's arm pulled him out of his memories. He was still at the police station, facing more questions.

"Ready to go back over this, Parker?" Nikki asked, dropping her badge onto the desk in front of them.

"As ready as I'll ever be," he replied. "I've already told you and Jim everything I know. Nikki, I didn't have anything to do with this murder."

"I sure hope not," Nikki replied. "I like Kate. Always have. I'd hate to see her hurt."

"But not me, right? I mean, you already think I'm guilty, don't you?"

The detective gave him a blank look. "Not for me to say. I just follow the evidence."

Parker reached inside his coat pocket. "Then you probably need to see this."

"Oh, right. The thing you and Kate wanted to show us. Let's have a look." Surprised, Nikki glanced down at the two gaudy toy lockets inside the plastic bag. "Well, well, that does add a new wrinkle. Where'd you get these, Parker? And why didn't you show them to us right away?"

Parker let out a sigh and ignored the throbbing in his scarred right leg. "Why don't I start at the beginning?"

TWO

Kate put the phone down then turned to her son. The expectant look on Brandon's face broke her heart. But she couldn't lie to him. "That was your daddy."

Brandon jumped up and down, clapping his hands. "Is he coming to my birthday party? Is he?" It was almost a month before Brandon's birthday, and it was all he could talk about.

Kate took Brandon by the hand, leading him to the small round breakfast table centered under the bay window. "I'm sorry, honey. He can't take time away from work."

Considering Dexter had finally found a new job after being unemployed for five months, Kate could almost sympathize with her ex-husband. She wanted to believe he had long-term, unbreakable plans, but she knew he was more likely planning to go to some sports event or a rock concert instead. Dexter still had a lot of growing up to do. He hadn't asked for joint custody of their child because he didn't want to deal with fatherhood, even part-time. He just didn't want to have a family at all.

"But he promised," Brandon said, his bottom lip beginning to quiver. "How come he misses everything? He missed Christmas, 'member?"

"I remember," Kate said, taking her son onto her lap. "Daddy lives far away now, so it's hard for him to make arrangements. But he loves you, you know. And I'm thinking he'll send a nice present even if he can't be here." She'd see to that herself, just as she always did.

Brandon pressed his head against her fleece bathrobe. "Why can't he just *bring* the present? Then I could have my daddy here, too. Like we used to be."

Kate knew Brandon wanted his family back together. Had she been wrong to do this to her child? She'd certainly tried to make her marriage work; she'd prayed about it, consulted her minister back in Nashville, even begged Dexter to go to counseling with the minister. But in the end, Dexter hadn't wanted to do that. He'd simply decided he had to have his freedom. And now, it seemed as if his son didn't matter to him either. Since they'd been back in Magnolia Falls, Dexter had called Brandon only a few times and had seen him even less.

But it mattered to Kate. She glanced out the window to the street. She'd been lucky to find this little cottage in the older part of Magnolia Falls, not far from the college campus. Here the streets were lined with moss-draped live oaks, age-old magnolias and crape myrtles. But her backyard wasn't really big enough to hold a birthday party, and her budget didn't allow for having a party at the fun-filled pizza place out on the interstate. She debated asking her mom to host the party, but Grace Duncan did more than her share of babysitting when Kate had to work extra shifts or stay late at the hospital.

And besides, Grace would turn what should be a fun time into some sort of formal, stuffy event.

"What we need is a big yard for your party," Kate said. "Like a park or a nice garden, maybe."

Brandon perked up at that, his eyes going bright. "Nana Grace says Mr. Parker Buchanan has the biggest yard in the county. She says his garden is supposed to be real pretty. I heard her talking 'bout it with Mrs. Welch from church. Maybe we could borrow his yard."

Wishing her well-meaning but gossip-loving mother hadn't spilled the news that the Patchman creator lived about eight miles from them, Kate looked down at her son. "Oh, honey, Mr. Buchanan is a very busy man. And he doesn't like visitors on his estate."

Which is why she'd hesitated even to try to track Parker down since the class reunion months ago. Each time his name came up amongst her friends, Kate tried to change the subject. By not getting back in touch, Parker had made it clear he didn't want to be bothered. Not even by an old classmate. And not even a murder investigation could change that, since it had been rumored that he'd balked when everyone attending the reunion had had to submit statements to the police.

Parker Buchanan might live in Magnolia Falls, but he was apparently off-limits to everyone in town. He hadn't even tried to call Kate after they'd reconnected at the reunion. But then, she hadn't made any effort to keep in touch with him either. She told herself that was because she was a busy working mom and distracted by all the strange happenings around the college campus lately.

"If we asked nice though?" Brandon said, his eyes widening. "You always say to use manners."

Kate had to smile at that. "Yes, manners are important, but asking someone for the use of their home isn't very polite."

"Even if we say please?"

Brandon's innocence never ceased to amaze her. But she also worried that her son would get hurt if he got grand ideas about meeting the famous Parker Buchanan. Yet Parker had said at the reunion that he'd like to meet Brandon.

With all the scandal following the identity of the body buried on the campus grounds, everyone was a bit skittish. The media had tried to get comments from the entire class, including Parker. But she reminded herself again, he wasn't talking to anyone, let alone the media, about his relationship with Josie.

Even though she hadn't seen Parker again since that night, maybe now was not such a good time to get in touch with him. Or maybe it could be the best time, she couldn't help thinking. Planning her son's birthday party would help take Kate's mind off that grisly discovery, at least. But what about Parker? Could he use a distraction, too? It just might work.

If she used her manners, of course.

"Tell you what," she said as she placed Brandon on his feet. "You finish getting ready for school and I'll see what I can do. I'll try to find a special place for your party, I promise."

"At Mr. Parker's?"

"I didn't say that. But we'll have to see. Don't get your hopes up, okay?"

Brandon nodded. "'Kay. But I'm gonna pray about it."

Another of her mother's phrases Brandon had picked up. Praying about things was a good idea, if you didn't pray for the *wrong* things, of course.

"Dear God," she said as she picked up Brandon's empty cereal bowl, "if You can see fit to help me make my son's ninth birthday special, I would so appreciate it."

And in the meantime, Kate would give Parker a call. After all, another one of her mother's phrases was "I can do all things through Christ who strengthens me, but I have to make the effort to be strong in Christ." Kate certainly knew that particular piece of wisdom firsthand. She could only depend on God's grace and her own strength to take care of her son.

Now, if only Parker Buchanan would see fit to make Brandon's wish come true.

Parker stopped drawing to listen to the phone message once again. Just to torture himself a little bit more, he reasoned.

"Hi, uh…Parker, it's Kate. Kate Brooks. You are one tough man to track down. I had to go through an agent and a publicist to get this number."

Only because Parker had given his publicist permission to give it to her, he thought. Just out of curiosity, and not because of a keen need to see Kate again, he reasoned. He had no idea what she wanted, but he wasn't ready to face her again. Not right now, just after he'd been hounded by the press and questioned briefly by the police about the latest developments in the murder case. He expected the police to question him again any day now, too.

"Anyway, I need to ask you a huge favor. Can you call me, please?"

Parker listened as Kate gave him her home number. He'd had it memorized since the message had come in yesterday, but he had yet to return her call. Or delete her message. His publicist didn't know what it was about. Kate wouldn't say. She just needed to talk to Parker.

A favor?

What kind of favor could she want?

Getting up to pour himself another cup of black coffee, Parker stared out into the night, his two loyal German shepherds, Patch and Daisy, following him across the spacious room. On the other side of his desk in the cozy sitting area, a fire crackled in the massive stone fireplace, warding off the last of the winter chill. His office was downstairs on the back of the house, overlooking the pool he'd had renovated this winter. The row of paned windows and doors across one entire wall gave him a stunning view of the sparkling water and the moonlit gardens. He could see the dazzling white of the dogwood blossoms just on the edge of the estate. Soon the magnolias and the moon vines would be blooming. The landscapers called it a moon garden, one where all the white-flowering blossoms shone luminous and ethereal in the moonlight.

The way Kate's pretty dress had shimmered the night of the reunion last summer.

And why was he thinking of that instead of calling Kate back? The very thing he'd so often thought of—having a conversation with Kate Brooks—now stood as a symbol of all that had kept them apart. And how many times had he thought about her over the last few months since their brief encounter at the class reunion? Just about every day, almost every waking minute.

But, as he usually did when he didn't want to face a problem, Parker poured his heart into his work. When he needed a break, he could take the dogs on a walk over his twenty-five acres, or go fishing down at the pond or just sit out by the pool, staring at nothing. Thinking of nothing.

Thinking of her.

"Okay," he said out loud as he turned back to his storyboard. "Get her out of your mind, man."

Kate Brooks came from a fine, hardworking middle-class family. Although she hadn't been as wealthy as some of their classmates in college, she'd certainly been popular. And since she'd grown up here in Magnolia Falls, she'd been on the inside track with the uppity society crowd.

Parker, on the other hand, had moved here in his senior year of high school and had never managed to fit in. His family wasn't rich. In fact, he'd lived in a house with his widowed mother and older sister on the wrong side of the tracks, so to speak. His mother had worked hard in the college cafeteria, but she'd insisted on Parker getting an education. So with money left over from his father's insurance policy, she'd sent Parker to college. She'd died a year later.

Now his only sister was married with her own family in Atlanta, but Parker made sure she didn't want for anything. He sent money to her regularly to help with her children's education. He was glad to be able to do that, since it looked as though he might not ever have children of his own.

Then he thought of Kate's son. Brandon. He'd told her he'd like to meet the little boy, though he certainly hadn't made any effort to do so since the reunion. But then, a lot had happened since that night.

Beginning with Trevor Whittaker finding a skeleton buried on the college campus. That kind of scandal sure put a damper on any type of reunion or party. Maybe that's why Parker hadn't bothered pursuing Kate. He knew she was here; knew she worked hard at her job. He didn't think she had time to date anyone, or at least he'd heard nothing to give him reason to believe that she did. He'd thought about calling her, but maybe he just liked the *idea* of Kate Brooks better than getting to know the real woman. Maybe he didn't want to risk that. Because that would mean she'd have to get to know the real Parker Buchanan.

Parker looked down at Patch. The black dog with the brown spotted nose stared up at him with big eyes. "She needs a favor," Parker said, shrugging. "What's up with that, old boy?"

Patch made a grunt deep in his throat. Daisy looked from her master to her mate and back, then whimpered low.

"Oh, of course you'd side with Kate," Parker said to the female dog. "You're a woman, after all. I know y'all conspire together, right?"

Daisy gave him a quizzical look, then slid down onto the braided rug next to Patch.

Parker wondered why humans couldn't be as loyal as animals.

The two dogs looked at each other, then back to Parker as if to say "It's not that hard. We love each other."

"Right," Parker said. "Love. That has to be in there somewhere, doesn't it?"

He stared at the phone, but he refused to listen to the message again. He didn't believe in love. And he didn't grant favors, even to an old friend.

This should be very simple, Kate decided two days later. It was a warm Saturday morning and Brandon was at soccer practice for the next couple of hours. And she was on a mission. Once she got something in her head, she plowed forward. Like moving to Nashville to become a country singing star. Or marrying the wrong man for all the wrong reasons.

But this was different. This was for Brandon. And Kate would do anything for her son.

Even if it meant breaking and entering, sort of.

"Got to move that mountain," she said, thinking of another one of her mother's favorite sayings.

She didn't know what had possessed her to wake up this morning with criminal intent in her mind, but something had urged her to go to extreme measures regarding Parker Buchanan. Okay, maybe it was because her son looked so dejected each time she mentioned his birthday. Since nothing she offered seemed to change Brandon's sad expression, she'd finally done a very foolish thing. She'd promised her son she'd talk to Parker Buchanan about at least coming to his birthday party.

"But that's *all* I promised," she told herself as she scoped the territory surrounding Brandon's gated estate. "I did not tell my son I was actually going to come here and confront the man himself."

She eyed the electronic gate and the six-foot wrought-iron fence. Well, she had tried reaching Parker the conventional way, but the man wouldn't return her messages. And he wouldn't answer the buzzer on the gate, either, even after she'd hit it for the third time just to be sure. Maybe he wasn't even in that big white house up on the hill. There was only one way to find out.

She was going in there.

Okay, so how exactly was she going to get inside this compound?

She looked around, thinking maybe if she found a tree near the fence, she could climb up and jump over. She saw an old oak, then tried to shimmy her way up the slanted trunk to the one low branch that could propel her over the high fence. Pushing through new spring brambles and old dead weeds, she managed to secure one tennis shoe to the tree, then lift herself up the ancient trunk. She climbed toward the protruding limb, then reached a hand out to grasp it. But the branch was limp and not as secure as it had looked from the ground, so her hand slipped, causing her to wobble backwards through the air. That only brought her tumbling back down onto her bottom, her hands rough and red from holding on to loose bark. Rubbing her raw palms against her now-soiled jeans, Kate stood back to stare at the graceful mansion sitting back away from the road. Maybe if she walked the perimeter of the property, she could find a way inside.

But after marching a few yards toward the woods, she realized the weeds and shrubs were too overgrown for her to be able to even find a hole in the fence. She had the thorns and beggar ticks on her jeans to prove it. And since the weather was warming up, there was a possibility that she'd encounter a rattlesnake or copperhead coming out of hibernation.

Frustrated, sweating and puffing, with her hair falling out of the haphazard coil she'd pulled together this morning, she came back to the fence.

"Maybe I can squeeze through those iron bars," she reasoned. Something told Kate she'd just have to *force* the issue with Parker, to get his attention at least. If she remembered nothing else about the man, she knew he was stubborn and full of pride.

Kate intended to break through all that, for her son's sake.

"Sure, like that's gonna happen."

Then an amazing thing *did* happen. The gate started to swing open. Glancing around, Kate wondered if there was a camera on her. But a delivery truck coming down the long drive from the house confirmed she was safe. Obviously, even a recluse like Parker Buchanan had to order supplies now and then.

So, taking the only chance she might have, she slipped through the open gate, in too much of a hurry to get in her car and drive through the normal way. She scooted around the partially open gate before the truck rounded the curve to the street, then hid behind a tall camellia bush until the truck was gone and the gate had shut.

She was inside Parker's beautiful estate. Looking around, she could see that the lawns and gardens were well-maintained and lush. A new springtime bloom covered everything from the great moss-draped oaks lining the drive to the shiny green magnolia trees waiting to blossom in a month or so. Soon the many azaleas covering the grounds would burst out in brilliant color. Kate could only imagine how beautiful this place would be during the spring and summer.

But she wasn't here to admire the scenery, she reminded herself.

"Now what?" she asked as she took a deep, calming breath.

Then she heard the dogs barking.

THREE

Parker glanced up from reading over some pamphlets and brochures the deliveryman had left. Patch and Daisy were going crazy out there about something. He'd let them stay out back after he'd shown the deliveryman the storage shed near the pool house. Watching them out the open French doors, he saw the dogs heading around the house toward the front.

Couldn't be the delivery truck. Parker had seen it leaving. Maybe someone else was at the gate, but he wasn't expecting anyone. Hurrying to check the security camera located above his desk, he rewound the tape.

Someone had definitely been at the gate, but he hadn't heard the buzzer since he'd been in the storage house.

Parker blinked. He couldn't be sure, but it looked like Kate. What was she doing out there on foot?

Wondering what was going on, he grabbed a cane and headed up the central hallway toward the big front door. Maybe Kate's car had broken down out on the road.

Hurrying toward the tall ceiling-to-floor windows, Parker checked the driveway but didn't see any vehicles. And Kate was nowhere to be found now, either. But he could sure still hear the dogs barking.

He went to the other window, then stopped, his hand on a sheer white curtain as he watched a woman sprinting across his yard with Patch and Daisy hot on her trail.

Parker shook his head. "Okay, there's a woman running across my property, with my dogs chasing her. Not good. Not good at all."

His heart slammed against his ribs as he headed to the front door, planning to call off his dogs before they caught up to her. Just as he opened the door, however, she came bounding up the low stone steps to the wide front porch. And because she was looking back at the dogs, she didn't see Parker standing there with the door open.

Kate Brooks ran right into Parker's waiting arms, causing him to lose his balance. Parker was propelled back to the floor with a skid and a thud, his cane going in one direction as his body slammed down with a jarring hit. The dogs caught up, still growling and panting as their paws hit wood and scratched hard after Parker shouted a command for them to halt.

"Ouch," Parker said once he was sure the dogs were secure. He steadied himself, then looked up, taking in Kate's falling hair and wide, frightened eyes. "It *is* you."

She stared down at him, her face red from running, her hands unsteady as she held them on his shoulders. "Uh, hi, Parker. Did you get any of my messages? Didn't you hear me buzzing the intercom by the gate?"

Before he could answer, Patch and Daisy inched closer, Patch growling and Daisy whimpering hello to Kate.

"Down," Parker said in a firm tone, causing both dogs to back off and turn in circles. "Sit," Parker said, afraid to move in case he was dreaming. But the pain shooting through his leg told him this was real. That and the woman in his arms. "Patch, Daisy, I said stay."

The dogs sat back to wait for his next command.

"That's better." Having settled his overly protective dogs, he centered his attention on the woman who'd just fallen with him. She smelled like spring and looked as though she'd been tossed by a strong breeze. He covered his joy and surprise with a glib reaction. "Let me guess? You were just in the neighborhood?"

"I did try calling you," she replied as she pushed up and sank back on the floor to stare at him. "And I did try to buzz myself in." Then she shot the dogs a wary eye. "Is it safe?"

Parker followed her gaze to the two dogs. "They're pretty harmless. Unless I tell them otherwise."

"Are you going to do that?" she challenged, that soft Kate smile on her face. "Since you obviously don't want me here."

"Depends." He got up, ignoring his throbbing right leg, then offered her his hand. "Do you come in peace?"

Kate took his hand only long enough to get herself up and steady, then she stood back, straightening the lightweight navy hoodie she was wearing over a T-shirt and jeans. "I only came here because you didn't return my calls." Then she watched as he managed to pick up his cane. "Oh, are you all right?"

"I'm fine. Just peachy." Parker couldn't believe she'd gone to so much trouble, but he didn't let on that he was impressed. "Did you stop to think maybe I chose *not* to return your calls?"

She circled him, her gaze sweeping over the long Queen Anne table and twelve matching chairs in the formal dining room just off the hall. "Yes, I thought that. But then, I also thought that even if you and I haven't seen much of each other since college, I still consider you a friend. And friends help each other out. Or are you too far above helping a friend now?"

Parker stood back, crossing his arms over his chest as he stared at her. "I have a lot of so-called friends these days, which means I have to be careful."

She pulled the elastic band off her hair, then tugged it onto her wrist, allowing all that pretty hair to fall free around her face and shoulders. "So you don't trust anyone, not even me? Is that it? Is that why you've been ignoring me?"

"I have to pick and choose," he replied, wondering how he could explain this without looking like a pompous snob. "I don't like to waste time and I especially don't like interruptions. And lately, with all the media attention about Josie's murder, well, as I said, I just have to be careful." Then he shrugged. "I didn't hear the buzzer earlier because I was out in the storage shed with a deliveryman."

"Right."

She didn't believe him.

"I'm sorry I didn't let you in."

"Well, *as you said,* we're all being careful these days." She moved around the hallway, her gaze taking in the antique walnut hall tree and the Chippendale secretary. Then she whirled around, disbelief and doubt evident in her bright eyes. "Look, Parker, everyone in town knows you're rich and famous now, so why don't you just get over yourself and let me explain why I'm here."

He leaned back against the secretary, a slight grin

forming on his face. No one did self-righteous indigna-
tion better than Kate. "So you're not overly impressed
with my success?"

"Oh, I'm impressed," she said, waving a hand in the
air. "I mean, who wouldn't be? This place is like
something out of a Hollywood movie set. But I just
never figured you'd go all cold and uppity to the point
that you wouldn't even return a phone call. This isn't
the press—this is me, Kate. I thought we were friends.
Honestly, why'd you come back here if you don't want
to associate with anyone?"

He wanted to tell her that he'd picked up the phone
several times, longing to hear her voice, wanting to find
out what she needed. But he'd never dialed her number.
Not because he was too uppity, but because he couldn't
risk getting too close again. So instead, he said, "I liked
the house." It was his standard answer when people got
too personal.

She nodded, pushed her hair off her shoulder. "So
you like your house, but not your friends? I thought we
reconnected at the reunion and then…nothing. Not a
word from my old buddy Parker. How rude is that?" She
wagged a finger in his face. "I think you like being able
to lord it over all of us."

"I might," he said, smiling at last. "So, is that why you
broke into my home, to let me have it for being so rude?"

She held up a finger again. "I didn't break in. The
gate was open. I kind of walked right in."

He nodded. "I see. All you had to do was announce
yourself."

"I did, several times. I mean, I buzzed that contrap-
tion. Aren't you listening?"

"I told you, I was occupied outside. The pool shed doesn't have an intercom. But I'll certainly have to remedy that."

"I figured you were just giving me the big brush-off. You don't want to be my friend anymore for some reason."

She'd probably figured right. Why was he so scared of this? Maybe because he couldn't stomach the thought of having her near, then losing her altogether? Which he was sure would happen.

He stared over at her, thinking that at least she had the guts to be honest with him. That was refreshing.

"What do you want?" he said, his tone brusque enough to hide his curiosity. She looked unsure and worried, and that was his undoing. "Kate, just tell me. If you really need something—"

"I need a favor," she repeated, her voice low. "Can we just talk for a few minutes?"

He nodded, turned toward the back of the house, then held out a hand to let her pass. "C'mon, I'll get us something to drink."

"That sounds good," she said, her sneakers squeaking on the hardwood floors. "Wow, this house is incredible."

Parker whistled to the dogs to follow, then watched her face, seeing his home through her eyes for the first time. He'd often wondered what Kate would think of his house. Would she like it? Or would she think he was being pretentious and overblown? How could he explain to her that it had been important to make this old house shine again? That he did believe in tradition and family, in spite of not having those things himself? This place had been broken and abandoned, crippled much in the same way he felt at times.

Healing this house had helped heal him. A little bit at least.

She turned as they reached his office, bending down to pet the dogs. "What are their names?"

"Patch and Daisy. They've been with me since I came back."

"Watchdogs?"

He nodded. "Sort of. And for companionship." At her raised brow, he added, "They're loyal and unassuming. They don't expect much from me. And they rarely talk back when I'm musing out loud."

She mumbled sweet nothings to the two animals, winning them over completely, then watched as they moved past her to the open doors out onto the terrace. Spinning back around toward Parker, she said, "Is this where you work?"

"This is it," he said, suddenly feeling as unsure as she seemed. So he just stood there with one hand resting on his cane, watching as she moved around the big room. He enjoyed the way her eyes grew wide with each new discovery, the way she smiled as she touched an artifact or read over some of his framed original comic strips.

Then she lifted her chin, listening to the soft music playing through carefully hidden speakers. "You always did like Mozart."

He was surprised but pleased that she remembered. "Helps me to relax."

She turned at his desk and the sight of her centered there amongst his most intimate possessions did something crazy to his heart. All of his circuits were going into overload. Telling himself he just wasn't used to company or such interesting distractions, he took his time enjoying this surprise visit. Then he remembered his manners. "I'll go get that drink? Water or coffee?"

"Water sounds good."

"Be right back."

"Can I come?" she asked. "I mean, I'd love to see your kitchen." Then she giggled. "I guess I'd love to see the entire house."

He nodded, his heart twisting with a painful kind of joy. Kate was here in his house and he couldn't think of a single thing to say.

In the end, she put him at ease in that Kate way he remembered. She laughed and chatted and commented on his expensive cooking pots and gourmet kitchen.

"I can't cook," she explained with a shrug. "Thank goodness for the microwave."

Parker didn't tell her that he enjoyed cooking and was pretty good at it. Maybe one night he'd have Brandon and her over for a good meal. Maybe. He'd been considered a nerd in college, so he didn't want to come off as one now.

He handed her the mineral water in a crystal goblet with a twist of lime. "Here you go."

"Wow, fancy."

He lowered his head, mentally kicking himself for showing off. But then, he had crystal goblets now. Might as well use them for company. Of course, he was also blowing any chance he had of seeming macho, either.

"I think you're the first," he said to cover his discomfort.

She blinked. "Excuse me?"

"My first official guest."

"You're kidding, right? How long have you lived here?"

"A few years."

"And you haven't had any guests?"

"My sister and her family come for visits now and then, but no one from…the old days."

"Probably good right now," she said, sipping her water.

"You mean with all that's going on?" He shrugged. "I do get the local paper."

"Yes." Her expression shifted from quizzical to wary. "It's just horrible—Trevor finding that body, then we find out it's Josie Skerritt. That, and all of this point-shaving business with Professor Rutherford and the basketball team. Then Cassie's brother, Scott, being found dead because he was investigating it—well, it's really put a damper on things around the college campus."

Parker remembered reading about the point-shaving scandal at the college. Apparently Cassie's brother, Scott, a local reporter, had stumbled across a point-shaving scheme involving the basketball team years ago, one that had caused Scott to have an accident when he was playing. It had ruined his hopes for an NBA career. Scott's sister, Cassie, and a professor named Jameson King had broken the case but hadn't solved Scott's murder.

Did he see a question looming in her pretty eyes? Did she remember that he and Josie had been close once? "Have they gotten any new leads yet?"

"Not that I know of," she said, her finger tracing the delicate design of the goblet. "I guess you've heard about as much as me. They're worried now about the baby, since they haven't found anything to indicate the baby died with her. We're trying to find our own answers. That's why we're trying to track down everyone. Steff and Dee are cooperating with the police on the PR. There's an alumni Web site set up to track our class—"

"Is that why you're here?" Parker asked, his insides going cold. "Did one of your friends or the police send you to get information?"

"No," she said, shock registering on her face. "Parker, honestly, I was just trying to catch you up on things." Slamming her glass down, she said, "And no, that's not why I'm here. But this is silly, so never mind, just never mind, okay?"

She turned to leave, but he caught her arm with one hand. "Kate, hold on." He put down his lukewarm coffee then turned toward the hallway. "Let's go sit by the pool and you can tell me the real reason you're here."

She followed him in silence, but Parker had to wonder if she'd come here on some sort of fishing expedition. Did she think he might know something about that body? Was that the favor she needed—to get information out of him for the police or her sorority sisters? But then, the police had questioned him just as they'd questioned everyone, and they knew where to find him.

He waited as she sank onto a white wrought-iron chair, then he sat down across from her, propping his feet on a matching table. Trying not to wince as pain hit his leg again, he said, "Okay—I'm done with the niceties, and I'm sorry if I seemed rude. What kind of favor do you need?"

He hated the hurt expression on her face. At first, she just looked at him as if she hoped to figure him out. Then she said, "I guess I shouldn't have come here. I should have taken the hint when you didn't call me back. It's obvious you don't want to be bothered." She stood up. "I'd better just go."

Parker stood, too. "No, sit down, please. I said I'm sorry if I was rude earlier, but I have some pretty obsessive fans and you have to admit you went to extreme measures to get to me. But you're here now, so talk."

She looked embarrassed. "I was desperate."

He rubbed a hand down his chin. "Oh, that sure makes me feel better."

"No, I didn't mean it that way," she replied, her blush becoming. "I— It's for Brandon."

Parker gently pushed her back into her chair, his entire stance changing. "What do you need?"

Her expression changed, too, at that simple statement. "You like children, don't you? I mean, you must since you write comic books geared toward children. And your characters are so vivid, so…inspiring. The lessons in your stories are universal and simple, but good examples."

He did like children, but more importantly, he liked Kate, and now that he knew this favor involved Brandon, he really wanted to help her son. And he appreciated that she *got* his story methods, that she'd even read his stuff. But he wasn't used to people reaching out to him unless they needed something from him. And apparently, Kate needed something pretty badly.

So, to hide his own treacherous feelings, he turned abrupt again. "Get to the point, Kate." Lowering his voice, he added, "Please?"

She sighed, then crossed her legs. "Brandon's birthday is in a few weeks and we've been trying to plan something fun and different. You see, his daddy stayed in Nashville and well, Dexter isn't the most dependable man in the world. He's already called to tell me he won't be able to come the weekend of the party. Brandon was so disappointed."

Parker sat still, his fingers templed together over his lap as he thought about what it was like, not having a father around. He certainly knew that feeling. He also knew all about disappointment. Disappointment and disgrace sliced through him each time he reached for a cane. "What can I do?"

She looked at him then, really looked at him, her eyes so full of thankfulness and gratitude, Parker almost hated the light shining in them. He'd never want to disappoint Kate.

But her next request was going to make him have to do that very thing. Even as he listened to her soft plea, Parker knew he'd never have the courage to help her. He was still so afraid of letting her down, of being that disgrace he'd always known he was.

"What do you want?" he asked again, his voice low.

"Well, Brandon wants to have his party here in your yard, but I know that's out of the question. So I was just wondering if you could at least make an appearance at the party instead. It would mean so much to Brandon. He has all your comic books and most of your toy characters, too. But to have you there at his party, well, I don't think anyone could top that. Would you be able to come for just a little while maybe?"

Parker sat there with the sun shining down on his face, with the woman he so often thought about sitting across from him asking him this one simple request, and felt his world shifting. He didn't want to turn her down, but he had to. He wasn't ready for that kind of exposure, that kind of public scrutiny.

So he looked directly into her eyes and decided it would be better to hurt her now than to wait for her to hurt him later. "I'm afraid I can't help you, Kate. I'm sorry, but the answer is no."

FOUR

"So he turned you down flat, even after you went to his house and asked him personally?"

Kate looked across the table at Steff and Lauren. They were waiting for Cassie, Dee and Jennifer to arrive for their monthly get-together, this time at Kate's house. These dinners had started after the reunion had brought them all together again months earlier. But now, because of the ongoing murder investigation and how that had affected their whole class from Magnolia College, the dinners had turned into a kind of therapy session to compare notes and dispel any rumors, plus help ease their stress and worries.

"He turned me down, all right," Kate said in answer to Lauren's question. "Parker apparently has no desire to get reacquainted with any of his old schoolmates. Especially me."

Lauren unwrapped the cookies she'd baked. "Parker hasn't been involved with any of us since he moved back here. But he did send a framed original print of one of his Patchman comics for the fund-raiser, remember?"

Kate remembered. She'd hoped he'd be there himself that night, but he'd been a no-show. "That was nice of him, at least. And it did fetch a good sum. Plus, he gave a hefty check for our cause, too."

"Sure did," Lauren said, pushing the cookies toward Kate. "And he did at least come to the reunion, even if he didn't stay the whole night."

Steff laughed. "Yes, just long enough to eat and leave. He seemed uncomfortable the short time I talked with him."

Kate thought about the reunion and seeing Parker there. Seeing him and talking to him, but then he had seemed standoffish and uncomfortable that night. For a man with a bad leg, he sure could make quick getaways. "But he didn't stop to visit with any of us much, did he? I had to force the conversation when we did speak."

"But *you* were always friendly with him," Steff pointed out, a hand touching on her blond bob. "You went out of your way to be nice to Parker."

Lauren giggled. "Yes, even when we warned you that he was a nerd and a loner."

Kate shook her head. "Parker wasn't a nerd at all. He was—he is—a loner, however. And there's nothing wrong with that. He's quiet and intelligent. Just because he wasn't a big jock doesn't make him a nerd. If he was nerdy, I'd say he's certainly overcome that now. Besides, nerds are very fashionable in the dating pools these days, right?"

She saw the look Lauren sent Steff. Throwing up her hands, she asked, "What?"

"You're defending the man who insulted you," Lauren said, her head tilted.

"He didn't insult me," Kate replied. "Well, okay, maybe he did." She stopped, shrugged. "I don't know.

There was something in his eyes when he said no. So much regret. I think if I'd pushed, he might have caved." She glanced out the window. "But I didn't push. I just thanked him and left." Maybe because she *had* felt insulted. And disappointed.

Steff leaned forward, the carrot stick she'd just nabbed from a vegetable tray aimed toward Kate. "You care about him, don't you?"

Kate grabbed a celery stick, then dipped it into the freshly made ranch dressing Lauren had provided. "Of course I care about Parker. But since we haven't been close in over ten years—if you don't count me falling into his arms after sneaking onto his property, of course—what's the point?"

Lauren sank down in a chair to stare over at Kate. "The point is, you might have gone to Parker's house for more reasons than just Brandon's birthday party."

Kate pulled the clip out of her upswept hair, then recoiled it on her head. "Now why would I do that?"

Steff took a sip of tea. "Maybe because, just like everyone else around here, Parker might know something about this murder? Were you trying to find out more about him?"

Kate shook her head. "You know, Parker asked me the very same thing. It never occurred to me. Do y'all suspect Parker? Is there something I need to know?"

"No, not really," Steff said, shaking her head. "I just wish we *could* find out more information. What we know for sure now is that the body was identified as Josie Skerritt. And now we have that locket with a baby's picture in it that Cassie found near where Josie's body was." She shuddered. "With the hand still holding it. Horrible."

And the mysterious initials on it, a fact the police didn't want to reveal just yet. None of them voiced that, but Kate knew what her friends must be thinking. Could that locket bearing the initials P.B. have anything to do with Parker?

Kate didn't tell her friends that Parker had become very suspicious of her when she'd brought up the skeleton found on campus. Or that he had accused her of spying on him. "Parker knows about the murder investigation and the locket," she said. "He reads the papers and watches the news. And Josie was his friend. He's as upset about her death as we all are."

"Then he knows about as much as we do," Lauren replied. "But since he was more friendly with Josie than some of us, he might be able to shed some light on the situation. I'm surprised the police haven't called him back in for questioning."

Kate spotted Jennifer's car pulling into the driveway. Thankful for the reprieve, she said, "I'd better go help Jennifer with her chicken enchiladas."

"Thus avoiding the issue of your true feelings," Steff said, a grin on her face. She nibbled her carrot stick, her eyes on Kate. "What are we to do about the mysterious Parker Buchanan?"

"There is no issue," Kate retorted over her shoulder. "Just because some of you have found true love doesn't mean I'm going to follow suit. I'm not ready for anything like that, not yet."

"Okay, so Parker's not an issue," Steff replied, shaking her head. "We get it."

Not an issue at all, Kate thought as she greeted Jennifer at the door. She wanted to add that he was in no way a suspect, either, but she was afraid to voice that to her friends. It would raise yet another issue she wasn't ready to address.

Which was, did Parker know anything about Josie's murder?

Parker finished the last frame for the next issue of *Patchman,* then leaned back in his chair. It was late at night and across the room, the dogs were sprawled on the worn braided rug by the fireplace, snoring softly at each other. The fire had long gone out, but that was okay with Parker.

Long, lonely nights. He'd had his share of those.

But that's the way you like it, remember?

He studied the stoic face of his comic-book hero, wondering what Patchman would do in a situation such as this. Well, that was an easy one to figure. A superhero would rush in where a mortal man feared to tread.

Mainly, at a crowded children's birthday party.

Why had he told Kate no? And why was he regretting it so very much now?

Maybe because he always felt a rush of aching emptiness each time he finished a volume of *Patchman.* Maybe because he had only his work to console him on these long, silent nights. Maybe because Kate had been here, in his space, walking through his home and he could still smell her sweet perfume. And maybe, just maybe, because she'd left with such a disappointed, dejected expression on her face that he couldn't stop thinking about her.

Parker ran a hand over his jaw, fatigue dragging him down. His leg ached with the perpetual pain; his heart ached even more. He remembered Kate on another night long ago, about a week before the car accident had shattered his right leg and changed the course of his life.

He saw her standing near the fountain on campus, the first of the camellias blooming pink all around her in the crisp February night. She was staring at the shooting water coming from a cherub's bucket. But, as Parker walked by, she turned and smiled at him.

"Parker…hi. How are you?"

Parker adjusted his backpack to hide his nervousness. "I'm good. Just finished studying for my English Lit test tomorrow. Professor Rutherford. He gives new meaning to the word *irony*."

Kate laughed, the sound echoing out over the night like chimes dancing in the wind. "I've been studying, too. Were you in the library?"

He nodded. "You?"

She grinned, shook her head. "I was with…a friend."

Parker knew that look. She'd probably been with her latest boyfriend. Parker couldn't keep up, so he didn't bother asking. He was about to walk away when Kate's hand on his arm stopped him.

As if sensing his thoughts, she quickly amended, "I mean, I was with my friends from the Campus Christian Fellowship. You should come to our next meeting. We're planning a Valentine's party."

Parker enjoyed the little spark of awareness running through him with the same intensity as the water shooting out over the fountain. To hide that, he shook his head. "Your friends don't want me in that group."

"Now why would you say that?" Kate asked, her

eyes shining blue-gray in the moonlight. "Everybody's welcome."

He started backing away. "Not everybody."

Kate followed him. "You shouldn't be so hard on yourself. *I'm* inviting you, so that makes you welcome."

He smiled. "So, on your word, I'd be accepted?"

She tossed her long hair. "No, you'd be accepted because it's a Christian group. Christ reached out to others, so I'm trying to reach out to you."

He wanted to ask her why, but he didn't. Did she want him to join her group so she could get to know him, or was she just recruiting for her church group?

"Will you think about coming to a meeting? I think you'd be surprised."

"Maybe," he said, shrugging in the face of her earnest request. He didn't particularly like surprises. "I gotta go." Then he stopped, remembering his manners. "Want me to walk you back to your dorm?"

"I'd appreciate that," she said. "Everyone else left. I just needed a minute…to myself."

Wondering why such a social butterfly would need some quiet time, Parker saw a new side to Kate that night.

"Are you all right?"

She nodded, clutched at her books. "Just tired. And I guess I'm a little sad. We'll all be going our own way in a few months."

Parker didn't think he'd have a problem saying goodbye to good ol' Magnolia College. "You got big plans?"

She grinned then. "I want to go to Nashville."

"Really?"

"Yes. I know it's silly, but I love to sing and I think I could make it there."

"You do have a great voice." He should know. He'd listened to her many times in the college choir. He always managed to stumble into their rehearsals, but he also managed to sit in the dark in the back of the auditorium so she wouldn't notice him.

"Thanks," she said. Then she went quiet again. "What if I fail? What will I do then?"

"Don't fail," he said, wondering how someone as sweet and beautiful as Kate could ever fail at anything. She was one of those people born to a perfect life, it seemed. Popular, pretty, well-rounded and smart, Kate fitted in here, she'd fit in anywhere. But he did worry that such a harsh, competitive place as Nashville, Tennessee, might swallow her up and spit her out. He couldn't bear to think about that. "You just have to have a plan. And you need to be careful."

"My parents think I'm crazy," she said, turning toward her dorm. "And maybe I am. But I have to try."

"You can always come back here, I guess."

She gave him an almost hurt look. "You don't think I can do it, do you?"

"I didn't say that. I think you can do anything you set out to do…but I'd hate to see you get lost in Nashville." Which translated to "I hate to see you go. So don't go."

When she didn't respond right away, he asked, "Want me to leave you alone, to think about it some more?"

"No," she said, strolling along with him, her blue wool scarf wrapped in layers around her neck. "I'm fine now, and I appreciate your advice. You're a good friend, Parker. So different from all the other boys around here. It's nice to be around someone who doesn't expect so much from me."

* * *

Parker had never understood that statement, but he'd wanted to tell Kate that he did expect *so much* from her.

He expected so much, but he knew what he expected was a lot different from what Kate might be willing to give.

So he'd never told her his true feelings. He'd started to, both on that night and on another tragic night. But fate had gotten in the way.

And now, he probably never would tell her the truth.

Pushing the memories away, Parker got up to walk to the other side of his office. The pool's water shimmered in the moonlight. He'd had the heated pool installed for the exercise. Swimming was supposed to be good therapy for his leg. So he swam and he walked the grounds, limping along with his faithful dogs by his side, and he tried to tell himself that he would be okay. He was safe here, secure. He had money enough to take care of himself and his sister if she needed anything. Security. That was all he'd ever wanted or needed. He wished his mother had lived long enough to know real security.

He'd actually believed he was content—until he'd seen Kate again at the reunion, seen her and found out she was back here for good. Now he had to wonder what he'd been trying to prove, hiding out in plain sight, here in the town where he'd never really fit in. Maybe Kate had been right. Maybe he was just showing off and lording it over all of them. It certainly looked that way, since he'd been so quick to tell her he couldn't help with her son's birthday wish. Had he become so high and mighty he couldn't help a friend in need? Or was he just afraid of being truly exposed, flaws and secrets and all?

"A perfect opportunity and I blew it."

Whirling, his right hand leaning heavily on his cane, Parker looked down at Daisy. The dog lifted her head, curious.

Knowing that if anyone ever found out how much he talked to his animals they'd probably think he truly was an eccentric recluse, he spoke out loud anyway, "I guess I was horrible to her, wasn't I, girl?"

Daisy growled low in her throat.

"I suppose you think I should make amends, right?"

Another soft growl.

"Flowers? Yes, I guess flowers might do the trick."

Daisy dropped her head back down on her paws and sighed.

"Flowers it is, then," Parker said. "First thing tomorrow morning."

Then he took the elevator to the second floor, wondering if he'd sleep at all tonight.

She'd just dozed off, curled up on the couch, when the doorbell rang.

Jumping up to stare at the ticking cuckoo clock hanging near the small fireplace, Kate saw that it was only nine-fifteen. But after staying up too late with the gang last night, she'd worked an early shift at the hospital this morning and then taken Brandon to soccer practice. She was exhausted. But whoever was at her door didn't seem to understand that. She could hear a soft knocking now.

Rushing up the short hallway to the front door, she stumbled over miniature action figures, then peeked through the small pane of glass, squinting into the light from the streetlamp to see who was out there.

Parker Buchanan!

Slinking back out of sight, Kate ran her fingers through her tousled hair, then glanced in the round mirror centered over a small oak table in the entry hall. Swiping at smeared mascara and day-old stay-put lipstick, she groaned. What did it matter how she looked anyway? And what was Parker doing here so late at night?

She seriously thought about just ignoring him, but then, she'd always been too curious and impulsive for her own good—according to her mother, anyway.

So she opened the door.

To find him walking away.

He whirled at the sound of the creaking oak door. "Uh, hello. I thought—"

"It's kind of late," Kate said, amused and touched by the enormous bucket of white lilies sitting by her door. "Out doing some gardening, Parker?"

He looked sheepish, shifted his weight toward his elaborate silver-etched cane. "No, just wanted to give you these." He shoved the copper bucket of living, growing, sweetly scented lilies toward her. "The woman at the florist shop said she'd never known a woman to turn down lilies, especially Easter lilies. Said they should do well in your backyard, something about propagation…I don't remember. But she said if you plant them, they'll come back each spring. Besides, she was shutting the doors when I burst in and so I grabbed the first flowers I saw." He shrugged. "It took me all day to get up the courage to go and buy you flowers."

Thinking that was the longest monologue she'd ever heard him utter, and that this was the sweetest gift she'd ever received, Kate laughed as she dipped her head to inhale the vanilla-lemon scent of the exotic flowers. "I think the lady at the florist shop got it right. They are beautiful."

"Okay, then." He shifted on the cane, turning to leave.

"Hey, wait a minute." Kate held the bucket of flowers in one hand, then nabbed his lightweight leather jacket with the other. "You're not getting away that easily, Parker Buchanan."

He turned, looked down at her, a solid fear in his sea-foam eyes. "I just wanted you to have the flowers—"

"Yep, I can see that, since you drove all the way across town to give them to me personally. So, that's it? Now you're just going to walk away?"

His full lips curved in a wry smile. "I thought I might just *limp* away, yes."

"Get in here," Kate said, lifting her chin. "I can make some coffee. And I have leftover pie—Lauren's famous lemon pie. No additives or artificial ingredients. Pure lemon and very tart."

He ducked his head. "I…I guess I could eat."

Kate grinned as she ushered him into the room. "Brandon is asleep, but his door is shut. We can have a nice, quiet conversation." She motioned to him. "C'mon into the kitchen."

She heard the tapping of his cane as he followed her. Sitting the lilies on the counter, she turned to smile at him.

And took another deep breath.

Parker Buchanan was here, in her kitchen. Suddenly, the little room seemed to shrink even more. She knew he was good-looking in that quiet, brooding way. But now, here, tonight, the man radiated a kind of tormented charm that made her want to run to him and give him a long hug.

If for no other reason than to show him that she still felt the same way she'd felt about him in college. He was a good friend who didn't demand or expect much more than a few words of conversation now and then. Or so he had been.

But now…Parker looked at her with a new kind of expression, a demanding, questioning, almost arrogant expression that seemed to dare her to accept some sort of challenge. Now, *she* had to wonder if she'd ever live up to *his* expectations.

Confused and very much aware of him, she busied herself with making coffee and slicing pie. "Sit," she told him with a flutter of her hand. He pulled out a chair and sat at the round oak table, his right leg straight out in front of him.

"My place isn't quite as big as yours," she said, realizing she was nervous.

"It's nice," he said in reply. "Quaint."

Kate laughed and nodded. "That's a good word for it."

"But it's your home."

Something in the way he said that made her stop and smile. "Yes, it is, but I'm renting," she offered over her shoulder. "I hope one day I'll be able to buy something nicer for Brandon and me—you know, with a big yard and more room."

"I'd still like to meet him."

She turned then, set his pie in front of him with a thud. "But I thought—"

He looked up at her, his eyes quick-changing and captivating. "I know what you thought, Kate. And that's why I'm here. I wanted you to know, I've thought about it and…well, I'd love to attend Brandon's party."

Kate felt tears pricking at her eyes. Silly that this could bring her to tears. "Really?"

He nodded. "I have to be there, since the party will be in my own backyard, right?"

Kate brought a hand to her mouth, then sank down across from him without a word.

He looked anxious, embarrassed. "That is, if you still want—"

"Oh, I want you," Kate said, a blush hitting her skin. "I mean, I still want you to come to the party. But, Parker, are you sure? In *your* yard, at *your* house? Well, not a house, exactly. More like an estate—but we're talking about twenty kids, so are you sure?"

His hand on hers stopped her. His eyes on hers held her. "I'm sure, Kate. This time, I'm very sure."

It was in that moment that Kate Brooks realized Parker Buchanan had changed. A lot. And that the "easy" friendship she remembered had just turned very, very complicated.

This could get complicated.

The lone figure stood across the street in the shadows, watching. Parker had brought Kate Brooks flowers. The man had always been a hopeless romantic. What a pity.

Now he would be an easy target.

And so would Kate.

FIVE

Parker had almost forgotten.

"Here, I brought Brandon something, too." He pulled the rolled-up piece of parchment out of his jacket pocket, then handed it to Kate.

"What's this?" She unrolled it, then gasped. "Parker, he'll be so excited."

Parker sat up to stare at the sketch he'd drawn earlier that night, just before he'd given in to the crazy idea to go buy Kate some flowers. "I thought Brandon might get a kick out of having his own Patchman portrait."

"Oh, he will," Kate said, her hand touching on Parker's signature in the right corner. "Maybe I'll save it for his birthday. It's just two weeks away."

"Go ahead and give it to him," Parker said, thinking he'd draw a million of the same just to see her smile. She looked relaxed now, not as tired and weary as she'd seemed when she'd opened the door. "I thought…I thought I could draw some caricatures at the party…for the kids."

Kate laid the parchment aside on the table, careful to keep it away from her coffee. "I still can't believe you changed your mind." Then she lifted her eyebrows. "Why *did* you change your mind, anyway?"

Parker chafed under the scrutiny of her earnest gaze. How could he explain? "I…uh…I'm not exactly known around here for being sociable."

"So?"

He had to admire her direct, no-nonsense attitude. "So, this was a tall order for someone who likes to stay hidden away at work all day long."

She grinned then, causing his heart to do a few leaps and bounds. "I get it—you're afraid of a yard full of eight- and nine-year-olds?"

"Something like that, yes." He wanted to tell her he was even more afraid of losing what was left of himself to her. But he was trying to overcome that particular fear, too. "It kind of caught me off guard."

She nodded, got up to put their empty coffee cups away. "I do that sometimes. You know, rush in where angels fear to tread. Or at least that's what my mother has always said."

"You're bold and courageous," he said in his best superhero voice. "I like that in a woman."

Kate shook her head, laughing. "Yeah, right. I'm not very bold and I don't have a whole lot of courage. I just wanted to make things right for my son. And in trying to do that, I didn't think my plan through."

Parker could understand that. "True, your plan had a few flaws, but we'll make it better. We'll make it special."

"We?" She grinned, looked down at her hands on the table. "I guess I do need some help."

He had to admit it sounded strange, him using a word such as *we*. There had never been a "we." Since his mother had died and his sister had married and moved away, it had just been him. *"Me."* Alone and lonely. Ignoring that little surge of joy moving through his system, he asked, "So…when do you want to plan this thing out?"

Kate glanced at the clock. "Since it's so late, let's hold off on that. We have a place now and a major attraction for the kids. I'll get the invitations done. I'm way behind on that as it is."

"I could draw you a mock-up," he offered. "You could make copies for the invitations."

"You'd do that?"

"Well, yes."

She pushed at the hair falling around her face. "Parker, I can pay you for all of this."

He lifted a hand. "This is my gift to Brandon. Don't mention it again."

"Thanks," she said, her blue eyes luminous with unspoken gratitude. "I really do appreciate this."

"Show me a picture of Brandon," he said, simply because he couldn't take the intensity of her eyes. Was he doing this to appease his guilt or was he doing it to force the issue—to bring Kate close? A little of both, he reasoned.

She rushed toward the refrigerator, the scent of the lilies following her. "Here's one." Bringing the soccer picture to the table, she handed it to him.

Parker stared down at the smiling little boy dressed in the Magnolia College Tigers blue and gold, that same rush of awe and joy filling his soul again. "He has your eyes."

"And his father's lethal good looks and charm," she

added. "I came back here so he could be with family, since he took it pretty hard when his dad and I parted ways."

"What went wrong?" He had to know, had to understand how someone could hurt this woman.

"What didn't go wrong?" she said with a shrug. Then she sat back down. "Remember our senior year, right before you had your accident?"

He nodded, held his breath. He remembered all of it.

"You warned me about Nashville, about not getting lost there."

"I just hated to see you go."

"Well, I did my usual thing. I rushed headlong into becoming a singing star…and fell flat on my face."

"But you can sing."

"Oh, I can sing all right. And I had lots of chances to prove that in Nashville. But I fell in love with the wrong man and married him right away. When I got pregnant, singing no longer seemed so important."

"So you gave up?"

"I didn't give up, exactly. I let go." She rubbed a hand over Brandon's picture. "Dexter had high aspirations for me though, and he became somewhat of a stage bully. He started out as my biggest supporter, then became my manager. But his methods didn't exactly win over everyone in the entertainment business. He made some enemies, used some tactics I couldn't condone, and that created a lot of tension between us."

Parker watched her face, saw her expression change from relaxed to perplexed. "Dexter wanted the dream more than I did. After I had Brandon, he accused me of being lazy, said I wasn't willing to work. But I just wanted to raise my child. I had found another kind of dream." She shrugged, took Brandon's picture back in her hand. "So my husband found another woman. A rising starlet who was willing to go along with anything he proposed."

Parker saw himself mentally bashing the man's head against a wall, but quickly dismissed that image. After all, Dexter was still Brandon's father, he supposed. "So you left?"

"Not at first. I was in shock, but I was determined to take care of Brandon. I stayed in Nashville, but went back to school at night to get my nursing degree. Dexter did try to help out with Brandon, but after a while he had too many excuses—tours all over the country, an album to cut. He was always busy. Too busy for his own son." She sat back against her chair, then ran her hands through her hair. "So when a job came up at Magnolia Medical I jumped at the chance to transfer back here, to be closer to friends and family. I just hope Brandon won't hold it against me."

"We won't let that happen," Parker said with a lift of his chin. "You were right to come home, Kate."

She tilted her head to one side. "Maybe. But with everything going on around here lately, I'm keeping my doors locked."

"You don't feel safe here?"

She gave him a quizzical look. "I did, until they found that body on campus, and I've just been so worried since they identified it as Josie. Look at everything that's happened since—several of my friends have been threatened in one way or another by someone we can't pin down, Professor Rutherford was arrested for point-shaving and Scott's murder connected to that. And then there's the charm with the initials—"

"The initials," Parker finished for her. "Yes, I've heard about that. But we really don't know much. I still can't believe Josie is dead."

"You and she were close, weren't you?"

Did he sense fear in her eyes? Or just curiosity? "I was her friend. Not a very good friend, but I tried to reach out to her."

"Do you remember anyone wearing some kind of necklace with a locket?" she asked, her tone neutral in spite of her concerned expression.

"No," he said, getting up. He wasn't ready to delve into the past, not with Kate. "And I didn't come here to discuss that."

Her stunned look spoke volumes. "Well, you don't have to leave."

He grabbed his cane, then turned to lean on it. "Like you said, it's late." Then, because he didn't want her to think he was hiding anything, he added, "And all this talk about murder and threats can't be good right before you turn out the lights and go to bed."

"I told you, I keep the doors locked, so don't worry. And I doubt I'll be sleepy now."

He had come here on a whim, without calling first. Well, maybe some of Kate's impulsiveness was rubbing off on him.

"Be sure you do lock this door," he said, wishing he could just take her and Brandon to his house. But that wasn't possible. Yet.

"I will," she said. Then she let out a sigh. "You don't like all this scandal and intrigue either, do you?"

"Who does? Like you said, it puts a damper on things around here." He turned to head to the door, then pushed back around, only because he had to know. "Kate, do you think I had something to do with all this?"

She stared at him a long time, her expression hard to read. "No, Parker, I don't."

"But…your friends are wondering, right?"

"We've all had questions," she replied, her tone full of sincerity. "That's only natural. And we're all being questioned. The police need every lead they can find."

Parker wanted her to understand him, so he boldly touched a hand to her arm. "I can't explain the necklace or anything else about this case. I don't know anything, Kate. Josie and I were friends once, nothing else. And if the police get around to questioning me further, that's all I can tell them."

"I believe you."

At least she didn't pull away. Her skin felt warm and soft, even if she had doubt written all over her face. Parker resisted the temptation to pull her close, to ask her to believe in him always. But he didn't want to have to ask.

He let his hand fall to his side. "I'll be in touch about the party. Maybe dinner sometime next week? I'll even cook it."

Her surprise was pleasant this time. "That's right, you like to cook. You really are a superhero, aren't you?"

Parker shook his head, leaned on his cane. "As you can clearly see, I'm not able to leap tall buildings. But I do cook a mean hamburger." He shrugged. "I figured Brandon would prefer that over seared salmon or prime rib."

"And so would his mother," she said, her eyes filling with gratitude.

"I'll call you later then?"

"Okay." She opened the door for him. "And thanks again, for the flowers and the party. Brandon will be so happy."

Parker stepped out onto the little porch, but he didn't voice his thoughts. He wanted Kate to be happy, too. And he wanted to be the one to make her happy.

Kate shut the security door to the neonatal intensive care unit, her mind still on the vital signs of the tiny baby she'd been monitoring. The infant's proud parents were with him now, their eyes lit with both wonder and worry as they gazed down at the little guy they loved so much.

Thinking of Brandon and how excited he'd been to wake up and find the Patchman print on the kitchen table, Kate knew that same feeling of awe and love. She'd been so bold in seeking Parker out, but she'd done it out of love for her son. With all the disappointment Brandon had felt since the divorce, she wanted to give him something special for his birthday. Somehow, she'd managed to do that, and in the process, renew an old friendship that she'd missed. Was that so wrong, she wondered? She could be Parker's friend, but she didn't want to take advantage of his good graces. She wanted their reacquaintance to be real, to mean something to both of them.

We could both use a friend, she thought, doing paperwork and checking charts while sipping her coffee on what would probably be her only break for the day. The buzz and hum of the hospital played like an old familiar song all around her. She barely glanced up as a woman in a dark hat and black sunglasses walked into the small waiting area to take a seat in the corner. Even though no one could get through the doors just past where Kate sat without being cleared and buzzed inside the unit, relatives were always coming in to wait in the lounge just outside the doors.

Thinking it was nice to have some of her college friends back as friends and confidantes, Kate had to admit it was also nice to have a man as a friend. But she would take this slowly, let Parker set the pace. She'd rushed into one relationship head-on and without thought; she wouldn't make that mistake again. She only wanted to be his friend again, well, because she had always admired and liked him in college. Parker was different, studious and a thinker, a philosopher, who, the way she remembered it, questioned everything. Even God.

Are you going to let that get in your way? she asked herself. Her mother would frown on that. But Kate thought it was better to embrace someone who didn't trust God, rather than turn away. Wasn't that what being a witness to the Lord was all about? She would show Parker by example how having God in her life had helped her overcome her failures and get on with the good in her life.

Maybe Parker needed her as much as she needed him. Or maybe she was just grasping at straws.

"You sure are in deep thought, darlin'."

Kate looked up to find her mother, Grace Brooks Duncan, staring at her with a displeased look.

Kate stood up. "Mother, did we have an appointment?"

"Don't sound so formal, dear," the second Mrs. Duncan said, flashing her latest three-carat diamond in the air. "Can't a mother come by to see her working daughter once in a while? Your coworker saw me wandering around and said you were out here taking a break."

Kate heard a "humph" from the coworker just before she was buzzed back inside the unit. Deciding it would be best to distract her mother before Grace figured out that all the other nurses were both terrified and intrigued by her, Kate stood and took her mother's sable-covered arm. "Let's go to the cafeteria and get some fresh coffee."

"I don't want any of that watered-down hospital stuff," Grace said, her dark hair impeccably groomed, her porcelain complexion heavily powdered. "I just came by to ask you what in the world is going on."

In a hurry to get her mother out of the tiny waiting area, Kate brushed by the woman sitting in the corner, nodding automatically as the woman adjusted her hat then turned back toward the window.

Kate stopped. "Mother, I have work to do. Why don't you get to the point?"

"Testy, aren't we?" Grace said with a shrewd smile.

Kate loved her mother, and Brandon and his grandmother had a solid, loving relationship, but Grace didn't make it easy. After Kate's father had died a few years ago at the age of sixty, Grace hadn't liked roaming around all by herself in the big old Victorian family home near the campus. So she'd remarried—this time a retired judge, a widower with money to burn. Thatcher Duncan was a sweet, lovable man and Kate couldn't ask for a better stepfather and grandfather for Brandon, but she knew Thatch, as everyone liked to call him, put up with a lot from Grace. And yet, he loved her mother beyond distraction. Kate gave him points for that, because she also loved her mother, in spite of Grace's always *being* a distraction.

Right now, she had to find out why her mother

seemed in such a state and why Grace had deemed it necessary to come to Magnolia Medical for an unannounced visit. "Is everything okay at home, Mother? Is Thatch all right?"

Grace fluttered her hand in the air again. "Thatch is out on the golf course, trying to find out all he can about this scandalous affair at the college. I tell you, this town is becoming another Savannah, what with all these incidents and occurrences. Thatch will get to the bottom of all of this and I'll get the details of whatever he found out at dinner tonight. Which brings me to you, young lady."

Kate gave up on the coffee, then gently placed her overdressed mother in a chair, wondering what incident her mother thought she might be involved in. With Grace, every rumor turned into an "incident" or an "occurrence." That was how Grace described things that were too distasteful to imagine, but too good to pass up sharing with friends.

"I don't know what you mean," Kate said, lowering her voice as the woman in the black hat noisily flipped through a magazine. Trying to figure what her mother might have heard, Kate thought over the details of her dull life. She'd tried to keep a low profile since returning home, for Brandon's sake if nothing else. She worked and took care of her son. She hadn't even tried to date—

"Uh-oh. Mother, what have you heard?"

"Only that my daughter has been cavorting with that strange cartoon man who took up squatter's rights at Magnolia Hall."

"Squatter's rights? Mother, this is the twenty-first century. Parker *bought* Magnolia Hall."

"So it's true?" Grace said, her smile triumphant. "You *are* taking up with that man?"

Kate rolled her eyes, then counted to ten. "I wouldn't exactly say I've 'taken up' with Parker, Mother. But yes, I have talked to him a few times here and there." She didn't mention that he'd been at her house last night. Besides, Grace probably already knew that. "We were friends in college, and we're both back here now, so I'd like us to be friends again."

"A slippery slope," Grace said, wagging a finger in the air. "You must have a short memory, Katie."

Kate knew this speech. Grace believed Dexter Sinclair hadn't been good enough for her daughter and she had voiced that many, many times. While Grace loved Brandon completely and honestly, she did not like his daddy. Dexter was her daughter's "mistake." And she had made it very clear she didn't expect Kate to repeat that mistake.

"I remember everything very well," Kate said, tired of this same old lecture. "That's why I'm home now and trying to raise my son near family—and that means you, Mother. Can't you understand that I also need friends of my own, including Parker?"

"Oh, I'm glad you have the girls back in your life," Grace retorted, smiling prettily. "Such good girls."

"I can't argue with that," Kate said, letting out a breath. "But we're all grown women now, in case you haven't noticed."

Grace slanted a look at her daughter, always scrutinizing. "In other words, I need to mind my own business?"

"Is that possible?" Kate said with a little smile and a playful nudge.

Grace took Kate's hand. "Honey, I just worry about you, and well…there's been talk."

Kate's defenses went up. "About Parker?"

"Well, yes. You have to admit the man is a bit odd, living alone in that big old house. He's never even been married. He's practically a recluse. And comic books? Honestly, does that sound normal to you?"

Kate's soft laugh caused the woman across the room to look up at them through her dark glasses. "Parker isn't normal in the way *you* expect, no. He's just a bit eccentric, but I can assure you, I'm safe with him. He's nice and sweet and very successful. He redid Magnolia Hall completely, with tasteful furnishings even you would approve. And he's very generous. He's going to throw Brandon a big party—"

Kate stopped, put a hand to her mouth. This time, both her mother *and* the other woman looked straight toward her. Glad the whole town hadn't heard yet, at least, she sat silent, waiting for her mother's disapproval.

"What do you mean?" Grace asked, her skin going pale. "Has he met my grandson? Why is he giving Brandon a party? I could have done that. I asked you about it a month ago."

Yes, Kate remembered that request. It had come with certain stipulations such as an exclusive invitation list, with all the right people. Not the friends Brandon wanted to invite, but rather the children of influential friends Grace thought her grandson needed to be around. And her mother had insisted on some sort of bizarre formal theme with boys in suits and girls in dresses, as if Brandon needed a cotillion for his ninth birthday.

"I told you we appreciated your offer," Kate said

gently, "but…Mother, your style is different from what Brandon wanted."

"So my grandson wants this cartoon person instead of me?"

"Brandon is a little boy and he reads all the *Patchman* comic books, Mother. He has all the action figures, too. That's what he asked for, and since Dexter is going to be a no-show again, I went to Parker. For Brandon, Mother."

Grace stared hard at the floor for a minute, her lips pursed, then said, "Well, at least he's getting the real thing and not just some paper plates with doodles on them."

Kate had to laugh at that. "Indeed he is. Parker is being very generous." Then she leaned close and whispered, "And I think I can get you on the guest list."

"Oh, you're so bad," Grace replied. Then she whispered back, "Are you sure he doesn't have a mad wife locked in the attic?"

"Pretty sure," Kate said, glad they'd waded through all the pitfalls of her connecting with Parker again.

But her mother's next words took away her relief.

"Well, are you sure he didn't have something to do with that ghastly skeleton they found on the campus? I mean, are you really sure?"

"Mother, of course I'm sure. Parker was Josie's friend. We all remember that. But he didn't kill her. That's ridiculous."

Neither Kate nor her mother noticed as the woman who'd been sitting still and quiet across the room suddenly got up to hurry past them. But she had noticed them, and she'd managed to hear almost all of their conversation.

SIX

"This is the biggest house I ever saw, Mommy."

Brandon strained against his seat belt in the back of Kate's minivan, his big blue eyes centered on the majestic white mansion at the end of the drive.

"It's pretty big," Kate replied as she waited for the gate to open. Parker had given her a code when he'd called last night to confirm their plans. "And remember what I told you—no running and no touching."

"I 'member," Brandon said, bobbing his head. "But what if Mr. Parker tells me it's okay to touch something?"

Kate shook her head. "Then I guess it would be okay. But just be careful."

"I will." Brandon stared ahead at the house. "Look, there are the dogs you told me about."

Sure enough, Daisy and Patch were waiting on the long wraparound porch. When the dogs saw the van approaching, they rushed down the steps, then whirled to look back at the house, both barking wildly.

Parker stepped out of the front door, a smile on his face. He waved, then petted the eager dogs.

"It's him," Brandon said, already unfastening his seat belt. "It's really him."

Kate's heart swelled from watching Brandon's excitement. What mother wouldn't want to introduce her son to someone he admired, someone who had helped him fill countless hours with imagination? But her heart became hushed and quiet, too. What if she was just setting Brandon up for yet another disappointment? What if he became too attached to Parker too soon? Maybe she should have thought this whole birthday thing through a little better.

Taking in the broad columns and two-storied splendor of the massive house, Kate was just as impressed as her son. What woman didn't dream of living in such a house? This even beat the rambling Victorian she'd grown up in and her stepfather Thatch's stately Georgian town house in Savannah. And it didn't help that the man standing on the porch looked right at home here, as if he'd just ridden in on a big stallion. Maybe Kate should have worn a hoop skirt and bonnet instead of jeans and a sweater.

"Mom, are we getting out?" Brandon asked from behind her, causing Kate to glance around.

"Oh, I'm sorry, honey. I was just thinking."

"Well, can you think later?"

Glancing around, she smiled at her son. "I suppose I could do that, yes."

Kate opened her door to find Parker right there, his hand on the handle. "Hi."

"Hello," she said, hopping out. "We're a little early."

Parker grabbed her hand as she landed, her loafers hitting the pebbled driveway with a skid. "That's okay, we're ready."

Kate loved the little-boy excitement she saw in his

eyes. He seemed just as pumped about meeting Brandon as her son was about meeting him. Brandon had already slid his door open to run around the car, the friendly dogs right on his heels.

Brandon giggled as he pushed at the wet-tongued animals. "They tickle."

"Don't be rough," Kate cautioned. "You don't need to antagonize the dogs."

"They won't bite," Parker said, glancing down as Daisy and Patch took turns sniffing at Brandon's clothes. "You must be Brandon."

"I am," Brandon said, offering his hand with big-boy authority. His grandmother was adamant about teaching him manners, and Kate noted it seemed to be paying off.

Parker shook Brandon's hand with a grand flourish, his smile gleaming. "I've heard a lot about you, Brandon."

The boy giggled again, then became instantly shy. Stepping back, he said, "And I know who you are already. You're Mr. Patchman!"

Parker laughed, too. "Just call me Parker, okay?"

Brandon glanced toward his mother with questioning eyes. "Grandma Grace says I have to call adults Mister or Miss. Can I call you *Mister* Parker?"

Kate nodded. "Yes, you *may* call our host Mr. Parker."

Parker shrugged, then grinned. "Okay, then I'll call you Mr. Brandon in return."

That made both Kate and Brandon laugh, but Brandon seemed to like that idea. Satisfied, he started petting Daisy. The big dog's pink tongue flapped out in bliss, while Patch pushed at Brandon for his share.

"I think they like you," Parker said, looking up at Kate. "And they certainly do remember your mother."

"She got chased," Brandon said with a shrug. "But they didn't know her then."

"No, they didn't." Parker slanted a look at Kate. "Not the way we know her."

Brandon frowned. "*I'm hers,* so I know her the best."

Parker laughed, then tapped his cane, this one with a whimsical Patchman figure on the handle, on the ground. "Ah, so you do. But I knew her when we were in school together, before you were even born."

That seemed to elevate his mother to new heights in Brandon's eyes. "Wow, you never told me that, Mom."

Kate brushed at her son's hair. "Well, that's because even though Mr. Buchanan is now famous, I still remember him the way he was back in college—nice and quiet."

Parker made the "loser" sign with his index finger and thumb on his forehead, causing Kate to laugh out loud. In return, she made a "W" sign with three of her fingers.

"Winner," she whispered to him as they headed toward the house. "At least Brandon thinks so," she whispered.

"I hope I don't shatter his illusions," Parker retorted as the dogs and the boy took off ahead of them. Then he gave Kate a look that held her to him. "Or yours either."

She couldn't help but wonder what he meant by that statement, or why the look in his eyes seemed to be asking her to trust him. Then she thought back over her conversation the other day with her mother. Grace had only voiced what a lot of people around here thought. Parker Buchanan was a mystery, an enigma, a man who held himself apart from everyone and everything. But why? What did Parker have to hide? Was he embarrassed because of his limp? Or was he just using that as an excuse to hide something else?

"Hey, are you all right?" he asked her now as he led her up the steps to the open door.

Kate looked at her son waiting with the dogs at the door. "I'm fine. Just had a long week at work. It's so nice of you to invite us, though."

He nodded, but his eyes told her he didn't believe her simple explanation. "This business at the college still getting to you?"

Kate waited until they were inside before answering. "I guess so. I just want it to be over so I can feel safe again."

She saw the alarm in his eyes. "Has anyone—"

"No, nothing like that," she replied. "I'm just jittery. You know how it is—you hear all this creepy stuff that no one can explain and then you begin to imagine someone is watching you. And then with all that's happened recently with my friends—Cassie, Jennifer, Lauren…"

Parker glanced toward Brandon. "We'll talk later." Then he leaned close, his eyes going dark as cobalt. "You're safe here, Kate."

Kate wanted to believe that; she knew it in her heart. How many times had she run into Parker all alone on the campus, day and night? He'd walk her to her classes or back to her dorm, or take her to get coffee, then help her study while they sat on a bench underneath a street-light, and she'd always felt safe. Why should that change just because someone had gotten away with murder long ago? Someone possibly still amongst them, she reminded herself.

But not Parker, never Parker. Kate refused to believe that, no matter the rumors or the speculation. And she certainly wouldn't have brought her son here if she'd had any doubts.

She followed Parker into his big study at the back of the house, listening in amazement as he patiently answered all of Brandon's questions and showed Brandon the most recent editions of the *Patchman* series. Brandon hung on his every word, his eyes lighting up, his smile bright. When Parker showed him the design for his party invitations, Brandon rushed to hug Parker, wrapping his little-boy arms around Parker's legs.

"Thanks, Mr. Parker. My friends are sure gonna love this party."

Parker looked down at Brandon, then brought his gaze back to Kate, his eyes full of awe and wonder. Hesitantly placing his hands on Brandon's shoulders, he said, "You're welcome, buddy. I like a good party myself sometimes."

Kate realized at that moment just how much this was costing Parker. He was going out on a limb to do this— for her son. For her. She'd never forget his kindness, or the look in his eyes right now.

And she'd never forget the glow in her son's eyes.

If only his own father had been this patient and loving with him. And with her.

We were a family, she thought, wishing her marriage hadn't failed. But she prayed each and every day that God would grant her some peace on that subject. She didn't want to feel like a failure, but she did. Especially when her son missed his daddy. Maybe that was why she'd gone to such lengths to ask for Parker's help.

That, and the way the man intrigued her. She couldn't deny her feelings for Parker. They had always been a mixture of temptation tempered with caution. He was someone forbidden, because he was so different from the jocks she'd dated in college. And very different from Dexter, in both manner and mood. Where Dexter had blown all hot and cold and burned out fast, Parker was as steady as a rock, centered, loyal, with a quiet strength that she was just beginning to appreciate.

She watched Parker now, noting his crisp button-down shirt and dark V-neck sweater, his jeans and sturdy boots. He was handsome in an aquiline, hawkish way, his features as etched and shadowy as those of his Patchman character. In spite of his damaged leg, Parker seemed to be in pretty good physical shape. Kate didn't see him as handicapped. She just saw him as a lonely man who had a worn, wounded soul. What had caused him to be this way? she wondered.

"Mom!"

Her son's exasperated call brought Kate out of her thoughts. She looked up to find both Parker and Brandon staring at her, one with inquisitive amusement and the other with big shining eyes.

"What?" she asked, glancing from Parker to Brandon.

"Dinner," Brandon said, his hands at his hips. "Mr. Parker told you it's ready, and I'm starving."

Kate felt the heat rising up her neck. "Oh, I'm so sorry. Guess I drifted off again."

Brandon rolled his eyes, then let out an exaggerated sigh. "She thinks a lot."

Parker grinned, then held out a hand toward Kate. "That could mean trouble."

Kate hurried to catch up, conscious of his eyes on her. "And just what exactly does that mean?"

He guided her into the kitchen. "It means that when a woman starts thinking, a man is sure to be in hot water somehow."

"And you know this because?"

"Because even though everyone in this town thinks I'm some sort of hermit, I actually have had my share of heartaches concerning women."

"Really?" Kate couldn't help but wonder just where and when he'd endured heartache. "I don't recall you dating much in college."

She watched his eyebrows shoot up at that. "Maybe that was because *you* were too busy dating all those football players."

"Oh, you noticed?"

"How could I not?"

She felt the heat of his gaze and the implications of his words, and wondered just how much he *had* noticed. How much he was noticing right now? Kate had a feeling Parker Buchanan didn't miss much of anything.

"Let's eat," he said, his smile soft and reassuring. "After dinner, we'll talk some more—about everything."

"Okay." She didn't want to delve into her college days with her son listening. But she had a feeling Parker would hold her to that talk, and that he would want to hear about everything that had happened to her since they'd been apart. But she expected the same from him in return.

They walked across the gleaming hardwood floors of the entry hall and into the long, rectangular kitchen. This room, too, had a wall of windows that gave a good view of the backyard. A set of French doors allowed the night to shine through. Soft spotlights placed here and there in the garden highlighted the moonlit night and the budding dogwoods. Soon the massive azalea bushes would be blooming, too. Spring was just around the corner, but the nights were still cool here in northwest Georgia.

"I hope you don't mind eating in the kitchen," Parker said. "The dining room can be a bit stuffy and formal when it's just a couple of people."

Although he'd told her she'd been his first real visitor, Kate had to wonder if he'd had just a couple of people over now and then. Or maybe just a woman now and then? She didn't know why that should bother her, but it did.

"We eat in the kitchen all the time," Brandon offered, grinning up at Parker. "'Cept ours is not this big."

Parker laughed at that. "Well, having you two here makes eating a lot more fun, that's for sure." He lifted Brandon up onto a bar stool set in front of a long gleaming cherrywood counter. "I hope you like hamburgers, buddy. Uh…I mean, *Mr.* Brandon."

"I love 'em," Brandon said. He squealed with delight when he saw the official Patchman emblem emblazoned on their blue china. "But I've never had a hamburger on such a nice plate, not even at my Grandma Grace's house on the fancy table."

That made both Parker and Kate laugh. Kate sat down beside her son, glad they were eating in the wood-and-chrome kitchen instead of at the "fancy" table she'd seen in the massive dining room at the front of the house. With a fireplace nearby and the glow of track lights and candles all around them, Kate did feel safe in this house.

In fact, the only time she didn't feel safe around Parker was when he looked at her in that quiet, observant way of his. Only then did she feel completely exposed and afraid.

But she was not afraid of this man. No, she was only afraid of what her heart might be telling her *about* this man.

Two hours later, Brandon was occupied with all the toys Parker had in his game room on the second floor, going from the Patchman video games set up in one corner to the pinball machine centered on the far wall, the dogs following him back and forth.

"Did you never grow up?" Kate asked Parker with a laugh as he led her to a sitting area in one corner. "An elevator lined with Patchman action figures on the walls, this romper room full of fun, this house with all the grounds and the pool and the dogs. It's amazing. I'll probably never get Brandon to leave."

Parker thought that might not be a bad idea, but he didn't voice that thought. Not yet. "I guess a part of me never grew up, but you can relax—I'm no Peter Pan. All the toys that have evolved from the comic book, well, that's just a part of my livelihood. And I like to test all the products personally that bear my name." He shrugged. "And the elevator, a necessity I'm afraid. It's hard to get up and down the stairs sometimes. Same with the pool—swimming keeps me limber and gives me a painless workout."

Kate glanced at his leg. "Does it hurt a lot?"

"Only when I walk," he replied in a deadpan tone, not willing to talk about that particular subject. "The muscles get tight and the degenerative arthritis seems to be kicking in more and more lately, but I get by."

He waited as she sank down into a cushiony brown leather chair, then he sat down opposite her on a matching sofa. Reaching toward the ottoman between them, he poured coffee from a carafe he'd brought up earlier, then handed her a cup along with the chocolate chip cookies he'd baked last night.

Kate took a bite of her cookie, then let go a long sigh, her eyes centered on Parker with gratitude and what looked like amazement. "All of this and he cooks, too. Now *I* might not ever want to leave."

Parker had to swallow to calm his pulse. He wished she actually meant that. "Another necessity, the cooking. After my mother died, my sister and I had to learn to do a lot of things on our own."

Kate put down her napkin. "Tell me about your mother."

He glanced toward Brandon, the child's laughter drawing him, making him yearn for a family of his own. "She was a hardworking woman who did the best she could for her children."

"And?"

"And that's about it." Before she could ask, he said, "I never knew my father."

He saw the swift-moving sympathy in her eyes, but she quickly replaced it with curious admiration. "You've come a long way, Parker."

"Maybe." He drank some of his coffee. "But I'd say I've still got a long way to go."

"Don't we all!"

He expected her to ask more questions, but she didn't. Instead, she reached for another cookie, her gaze bouncing around the room.

"This place is like a child's fantasy come true," she said between bites. "Do you ever come up here on your own and play with this stuff?"

"No," he said, "at least not since it first arrived. It's just here."

He wanted to tell her it was here waiting for a little boy like Brandon to make it come alive, to enjoy all this in the way it was meant to be enjoyed. But he didn't say that.

"That's sad," Kate retorted. "I mean, you don't have to hide out here, you know. Why don't you get out more?"

He leaned forward to place his coffee back on the tray. "I might. Up until now, I've never had much of a reason to get out. I like my solitude, the quiet of this old place. I like my work. But now—"

"What?" she asked, her body seeming to tense as she waited for his answer.

The spin of the pinball machine sang through the night, followed by Brandon's laughter as he talked to the dogs. All foreign sounds to Parker, sounds that made him realize all the more how lonely he was.

"But now," he continued, trying to find the right words, "I think I might have two very good reasons to start enjoying life a little more." And because he couldn't resist, he reached across the space between them and took her hand. "Do you understand what I'm saying, Kate?"

He heard the sharp intake of her breath, saw the confusion, followed by hope, in her eyes. "I think I just might." She squeezed his hand and smiled over at him. "We can start with Brandon's party and see how things progress from there. How does that sound?"

Parker looked down at their joined hands. "That sounds good. Very good."

* * *

Out on the highway, beyond the towering black iron gates that kept the world away, a lone woman stood staring up at the glowing old mansion, her fists held tightly pressed against her stomach, her body shivering in the crisp night wind, as she remembered how Parker Buchanan had ruined her life. Now it was her turn to ruin his.

And she'd start with Kate Brooks.

SEVEN

"I'm telling you, I love pizza."

Kate shook her hair off her face, but the brisk wind only pushed it back. "I'm so sorry, Parker. I really thought baked chicken would be easy."

Brandon tugged on her coat sleeve. "Grandma says chicken *is* easy, but I guess her oven works better than yours, huh, Mom?"

Kate frowned down at her son. "Yes, Grandma's oven is perfect, and she does have a housekeeper to help her, you know."

"Maybe we need one," Brandon said as they entered the building then settled into a booth at Burt's Pizza. "I sure am starving."

"You're always starving," Kate retorted, her frown intact after a brief flash of a smile.

Parker remained silent, enjoying the way Kate and her son bantered back and forth. Even though she was not happy about ruining their dinner, which was meant to be her thank-you to him for throwing the party, it was obvious that Kate was a good mother. And Brandon was a typical little boy, all energy and curiosity. Parker didn't mind one bit that he'd been forced to go out in public just to have another evening with them. Well, maybe he did mind the way people were beginning to stare and whisper, but he'd have to get over that.

"I think I like pizza much better than baked chicken anyway," Parker said, hoping to get rid of the worried frown on Kate's face. "I say we get a big one, with the works."

"Mom likes mushrooms," Brandon told him in a matter-of-fact tone, his face in his hands as he leaned against the table.

Parker winked at him. "Then we'll order extra mushrooms, but only if your mom decides to smile."

Kate glanced up from studying the menu, then lifted her son's elbows off the table. "I just wish I hadn't burned the chicken to a crisp. The recipe said bake one hour. I did that."

"Looked like two hours, the way it was smoking," Brandon replied, his eyebrows winging up as he said it.

Parker grimaced to hide his smile. "Maybe Daisy and Patch will eat it."

"You think?" Brandon asked, excited at the prospect. "I bet they get a bad stomachache."

"Okay, enough," Kate said, glancing around for a waiter. "What's taking so long?"

Sensing her distress was more about their ruined meal than about waiters, Parker touched a finger to her hand. "Kate, it's okay."

He had to make the best of this just to show her he wasn't upset over the ruined chicken. He couldn't let her see his distaste at being in such a noisy, crowded place. But he had to acknowledge that he was a local curiosity, someone people would naturally wonder about, given his fame and his reputation as a recluse.

Kate put down her menu. "It's just that…" She stopped, her gaze falling across her son. "In Nashville, I wasn't exactly praised for my domestic skills, if you get my drift."

"Dad hollered about her cooking," Brandon blurted, his eyes losing some of their little-boy luster.

Parker sent Kate a look that he hoped conveyed what he was thinking. *Dexter Sinclair wasn't good enough for you.* Then he turned to Brandon. "Nobody is going to holler tonight, buddy. Let's get some pizza." He motioned for a skinny kid to come over and take their order.

After that had been taken care of, Brandon squirmed around. "Mom, can I go say hi to my friend from school over there?"

Kate glanced at a booth across the room where Seth Chartrand sat with his son, Jacob. Waving to Seth, she said, "You can visit for a while, just until our food comes."

Brandon nodded, then ran over to sit down with Jacob. Parker watched as the two little boys chattered away, then nodded toward Seth with his own hello.

"Brandon's probably telling Seth all about his party," Kate replied. "His friends are just as excited about meeting you and seeing your home as Brandon." She watched her son's animated expression, then looked back down at the table. "I hope things go smoothly."

Since she still seemed so mad at herself, Parker cleared his throat and tried again. "Are *you* excited about the party? Or do you wish we hadn't planned it?"

She looked across at him then, her eyes going wide. "Oh no. I mean, I'm excited, of course." Then she hit the heavy oak table with her hands. "I didn't want to say this in front of Brandon, but Dexter used to tease me about my cooking a lot. Well, he'd tease and then he'd get downright angry—I guess Brandon still remembers some of our arguments."

Though Kate wouldn't speak badly about Dexter for Brandon's sake, Parker had little respect for the man. "Angry? About a meal?"

She nodded, played with the end of her paper napkin. "Oh, yes. But in just about every arena, I'm afraid Dexter's expectations far exceeded my abilities. He couldn't forgive me for not being a success."

Hating her look of self-disgust, Parker said, "I've heard you sing, Kate. You have incredible talent. Maybe Dexter just wasn't the right manager."

She waved that away. "But I wasn't good enough. And you haven't heard me sing in a very long time, since you don't come to church."

Not used to this side of her—she'd always been so confident and sure and nonjudgmental—he leaned forward. "I don't have to hear you now, to know that you were good. And I'm sure you still are. You can't let a jerk like your ex-husband bring you down."

She ran a hand over her hair, then finished shredding her napkin. "I burned our dinner, Parker." Her shoulders slumped. "Why is it that I can take care of the tiniest of babies all day long, but I can't even boil water?"

He leaned forward, forcing her to look at him. "Why are you even comparing the two? Saving premature infants takes a lot of skill and talent, not to mention love and incredible patience, Kate. I'd say that ranks way over cooking a meal."

"But I wanted this to be special—for you."

"Being here is special," Parker said, his voice low. "Being with you and Brandon—that's the only thing that's important to me."

"But you don't like being around people."

He had to smile at her words. "It's not so much that I mind being around people. It's more like people don't like being around me."

"That's silly," she said, quick to jump to his defense.

"Is it?" he asked, his gaze flickering toward the next table. "Don't you see how everyone in here is staring? They think I'm some kind of freak. And now we can add 'person of interest' to that, since my name is being bandied about in connection to Josie's murder."

She shook her head. "You don't know that for sure, and the police don't have any evidence to justify that. And you *are* a local legend amongst the kids. They probably want your autograph, but they're afraid to approach you. So now you're the one having a pity party."

Glad to see she'd regained some of her teasing defiance, he nodded. "Yes, I've had one ten-year-long pity party, that's true. But I'm learning to let go of some of my regrets and bitterness, thanks to you and Brandon. I can handle things a lot better these days. Even people gossiping about me, or wanting my autograph."

She glanced around, then looked back at him before she exhaled a deep breath. "I didn't even ask you how you felt—about coming here, I mean. I know you don't like to be seen around town—"

"Alone," he added. "Before, I didn't like coming into town *alone*. But I'm not alone tonight."

She finally smiled, a soft lifting of her pretty lips. "No, you're not. Thank you."

"For what?"

"For making me feel better. I know this hasn't been easy for you."

"You're not making sense."

"*Me,* Parker. I'm not easy—I'm pushy and impulsive and I do these crazy things, even when everyone warns me—"

"Did they warn you about me?"

She nodded before she caught the motion. "Yes, I mean, no. I don't know. Like you said, people love to talk, to speculate. And here I've forced you to be exposed to all of that."

Parker looked around, sensing from the covert glances coming their way that they were still being scrutinized. "I'm doing okay, really. Let 'em talk." Hoping to cheer her up, he added, "I have nothing to hide, but you do."

"What do you mean?" she asked, shock registering on her face.

"You burned a perfectly good chicken. People tend to gossip about that sort of thing."

She burst out laughing then, causing several diners to look around. Seth noticed, too, said something to his son and Brandon, then strolled over to their booth.

"Hello," he said, shaking Parker's hand. "The wily Parker Buchanan, right here in Burt's, and smiling at that. This is certainly a first."

Parker grinned. "Guess you never thought you'd see me here, right?"

"Or anywhere else in town for that matter," Seth replied. Then he looked at Kate. "And how are you?"

"I'm fine," Kate said, smiling over at Parker. "I burned dinner."

"Oh, well, that explains it, then. Even a recluse like Parker has to eat, I reckon." Cupping his hands to his mouth, he added, "I've already heard Brandon's version. Very colorful—something about smoke detectors going off and a really bad smell in the house."

"My son exaggerates," she replied. Ignoring his grin, she asked, "Where's Lauren?"

"She has a big catering job tomorrow, so we decided we'd give her some space tonight. Now that she's taught Burt how to make an allergen-free pizza, Jacob can actually eat here."

Kate motioned toward Parker. "He's a gourmet cook, too. They need to get together and compare notes. Or maybe teach me how to cook."

Seth glanced from her to Parker, then back. "Oh, somehow I don't think Parker minds that you can't cook."

Kate looked surprised, then pleased. "Parker is a very polite and understanding man."

Seth grinned at that. "It's good to see you two together."

Parker brushed his fingers across the table. "I have to admit, I need to come into town more often. This place hasn't changed a bit."

"Some things never do, thankfully," Seth replied. Then he added, "I'll leave you two alone." Backing away, he touched on the table with a knuckle, then dipped his head. "Still no news from the police?"

"Nothing new since they found that locket," Kate said. "All we can do is wait to hear what significance the locket has to all of this."

The silence settled over them, despite the noisy restaurant. Seth lifted his chin. "This has been tough on all of us, especially Lauren. We certainly had a couple of close calls with a stalker, but at least we cleared up some of that."

"The babysitter, of all people," Kate interjected.

"Yeah, just a jealous kid but she claims she didn't take Lauren's laptop from her car during all of that mess but it hasn't turned up anywhere." Seth lowered his voice. "That's the part that scares me. What if it was someone else—the person who knows about this murder?"

Parker glanced over at Kate. "We'll all rest easier when the police find out who's behind it."

Kate let out a sigh, her doubtful gaze touching on Parker. "Maybe we'll know something soon."

Seth looked back at the giggling boys. "I guess I'd better get back before those two start a food fight with the breadsticks," he said, motioning to Jacob and Brandon. "See you later."

"Send Brandon back over here so you can enjoy your meal," Kate called after him.

In the next minute, Brandon hurried to their table just as the waiter brought their pizza.

"Let's eat," Parker said, his gaze holding Kate's. Her worried expression changed as Brandon scooted into the booth beside her. Smiling at Parker, she changed the subject seamlessly, for Brandon's sake he guessed. "I can't believe you haven't eaten here since college."

"Oh, I've had lots of pizza from Burt's," he replied. "I have the deliveryman on speed dial. Daisy and Patch know him very well."

She laughed out loud again, her smile beautiful as her mood lightened.

Parker concentrated on the woman and boy seated across from him, even while he could feel the patrons of Burt's concentrating on him. And probably spinning even more tales for the rumor mill.

But Parker knew in his heart that he'd done the right thing, reconnecting with Kate. In the last few weeks, his life had gone from bleak and lonely to upbeat and hopeful.

And he prayed to God that didn't change anytime soon.

Even though he was out of practice and afraid God might not hear his prayer.

"He's out," Kate whispered, closing Brandon's door behind her. Motioning to Parker, she guided him back toward the den. "Have a seat."

"Are you sure?" he asked, his hands at his side, his lion-head cane tucked under his elbow. "Don't you have to get up early?"

"I have the late shift tomorrow," she said, glad she'd be able to spend more time with Brandon before school in the morning. "Brandon gets to enjoy a long afternoon with his grandmother Grace."

"Are they close?"

"Oh, yes. My mother spoils him even while she tries to make him conform to her image of a proper gentleman. And Judge Duncan, well, he seems to love Brandon as much as he does his own grandchildren. I'm blessed to have their help."

"It's good that Brandon has extended family. I don't get to see my sister and her kids very much, but I can't help spoiling them when I do."

Kate could just see Parker arriving for Christmas with a truckload of gifts. She'd have to be careful that he didn't offer too much to Brandon.

She watched as Parker sank down beside her on the couch, noting how he favored his right leg. "Is your leg bothering you?"

He stretched it out, then placed his cane on the coffee table. "I'm okay. It gets better as the weather warms up."

She shivered, looking out at the rainy night. "I think we're in for one more cold snap before spring finally gets here." Grabbing a cream-colored chenille throw, she wrapped it around her shoulders. "That's better."

Parker sat looking at her for so long, she finally waved a hand in front of his eyes. "Parker, are you all right?"

"I'm fine," he said, his fingers templed together in his lap. "I guess I just can't believe I'm here with you."

Surprised and aware of how close he was, Kate laughed. "And why is that so hard to believe?"

"Oh, you know…the whole thing—college, drifting apart, life. I guess that reunion brought to light a whole lot of things I'd been trying to deny."

Kate's heart lurched against her insides. "What kinds of things?"

He shifted, settled back against the burgundy cushions scattered on the couch. Then he reached for her hand. "You and me, Kate. Did you ever wonder about how things might have gone between us if I hadn't had the accident?"

Confused and a bit rattled by the warmth of his touch, she didn't know how to answer that. "I don't know. I was so wrapped up in getting to Nashville, I guess I never imagined anything else after college." Then she tugged at her hair with her free hand, letting it fall away from the tortoiseshell clip that held it. "And if I recall correctly, you didn't like having visitors when you were going through all your surgeries. So just for the record, I did try to see you."

"I know you did," he admitted as he looked at their joined hands. "My sister told me you came by the hospital every day."

Kate lifted her chin. "I think that's why I finally went into nursing. I felt so helpless, knowing you needed me and I couldn't do anything to help you. Or at least, you wouldn't let me do anything."

He leaned close then, his eyes going emerald in the lamplight. "I don't think I could have handled your pity."

Kate's heart went out to him. "So you pushed me away."

"I did it only because I knew you were better than me, Kate. Or you deserved better, anyway, and you had your life mapped out already. I didn't have much to offer."

"But what about our friendship? You didn't want to keep that, at least?"

He must have sensed the hurt in her voice, in her eyes. He didn't answer for a minute, but she could feel by the way he brushed his thumb over her knuckles that he was having a hard time explaining this to her.

Finally, he reached up his other hand to touch her hair, his fingers trailing through the strands, his eyes holding her gaze. "I wanted more than just friendship, Kate. I wanted more than you could give."

Kate heard the silence in the room, heard his sharp intake of breath, just as she heard the pulse of her own heartbeat pounding inside her head. And she thought about how she'd always had a thing for Parker, how she wished he'd been more open with her back then. She'd held this secret crush so close in her heart, that even now she was having a hard time admitting it. And she realized, if Parker had pushed her for something more back then, she probably *would* have run away.

Tears pricked at her eyes as she saw the truth at last. "You didn't want to hold me back."

He placed his other hand on her hair, holding her like something precious, captivating her with the firm gentleness of his touch. "I didn't have the right to hold you back."

Kate's impulses kicked in, making her brave. "And now?"

He moved closer. "And now, here we are. We've found each other again. Do you believe in second chances?"

She could only nod. She felt so exposed, it hurt to speak. But she didn't have to. Parker could read it in her eyes.

He held her there, his gaze moving over her as if he were trying to memorize her features. "Do you believe we could be more than just friends?"

Again, she nodded. And this time, she knew the answer. "Oh, yes."

His smile was bittersweet, his kiss soft and promising. His very gentleness shattered her, while his quiet strength steadied her. And she knew what she'd hidden so deeply in her heart all these years had now been revealed.

All those years ago, how many times had she purposely waited at certain spots on the campus, knowing Parker would come along and find her, knowing that he'd cheer her up, make her laugh and brighten her day? Knowing that if she'd made the first move, Parker would have been the one.

And now she'd come back to Magnolia Falls, searching for something she'd never been able to find in Nashville. While Parker Buchanan, so very mysterious and such a paradox, was right here, waiting for Kate to come home.

Just as she'd been waiting for him to come out of hiding and find her.

EIGHT

It just wasn't fair.

The woman sat on a bench in a remote part of town, away from all the activity at Magnolia College. She stared at the winding river moving off in the distance, wondering why she couldn't just float away and disappear forever.

They all owe me, she thought, bitterness gnawing at her. She had to do something; she had to come up with another plan. Something to get them off the trail. That stupid alumni Web site was going to ruin everything for her. And the one person she could always count on had deserted her. Who could she turn to now? Who could she trust to help her?

Not Parker. Never him. But Parker Buchanan, well, he *was* expendable. He had no reason to fight, no one to live for. Not like she did. Parker didn't even seem capable of love. But he might be capable of murder. Twice, if she had her way.

He'd ruined her life. Now it was time to return the favor.

She picked up the brand-new prepaid cell phone she'd purchased in another town. They wouldn't be able to trace her on this one. But she'd only use it this once, just in case.

Her pulse quickening, she dialed the Magnolia Falls police station. Then she whispered into the phone. "I have a tip about the college murder. I think I know who buried that body there ten years ago. And I think I know why."

Kate didn't know why she felt this way. Glancing around, she checked the hospital parking lot, a cold shiver working its way down her spine. No one was lurking in the bushes; no one was following her. The neonatal staff had guards to escort them to their cars, since they had to deal with ex-husbands and angry drugged-up boyfriends a lot, and tonight was no exception. Glad for the rule, she smiled over at the man walking with her. "How you doing tonight, Clarence?"

"Right as rain, Ms. Brooks," the older man said, his chocolate-colored eyes brightening. "How 'bout you?"

"Couldn't be better," Kate replied, feeling reassured as he waited for her to unlock her car door. "Thanks so much." After a little more small talk and a good-night wave, she got inside and breathed a sigh of relief.

Why did she feel as if she were being watched? Maybe she was just imagining things after what Dee had been through over the last few weeks. It was reasonable, since they'd all been jittery and frightened for months now.

But this nagging sensation had started a couple of days ago, when she was at the superstore getting supplies for Brandon's birthday party. The busy store had been filled with people milling about, but Kate had been alone on the party-goods aisle. At least, she thought she'd been alone. Then she'd turned to catch a glimpse of a woman hurrying away. Where had she seen that woman before?

That thought had nagged at her earlier in the day, when she left the hospital to have lunch with her mother. She'd sensed someone nearby, then a car had sped away. A car she didn't recognize.

She'd even mentioned it to Grace at lunch.

But her mother only tried to soothe her nerves. "Well, goodness, darlin', we're all a bit skittish right now. The more I read in the papers, the more I worry for all of us. But Thatch assures me we're safe. At least he installed a security system in our house right after we got married." Then she leaned forward, her chicken salad hanging onto her fork. "You and Brandon could come and stay with us until this is all over."

"No," Kate replied, thinking she loved her mother but they both needed lots of space. "I'm not really in fear, Mother. I just get these weird sensations. You know how the hair on the back of your neck can stand straight up?"

"Okay, you're scaring me, honey," Grace replied.

Worried she was sounding crazy, Kate backtracked. "Oh, you're right. It's silly. I'm fine. We're fine. So don't worry about me."

Grace looked doubtful. "Well, my offer stands—if you need a place to stay for a while. And in the meantime, you keep a close watch on things around your house."

Kate thought about that now as she left work. So far, she hadn't felt anything amiss around her house. But she certainly remembered all the weird things that had taken place since the discovery of that skeleton. Lauren's laptop being stolen, that creepy locket with the mysterious initials that the police refused to talk about, then Dee being stalked by Cornell Rutherford, of all people. Cassie was even shot at when she was trying to investigate her brother's death. It was all too much. No wonder her imagination was running wild.

Telling herself that she was both tired and a bit off kilter since Parker had kissed her, she turned out into traffic and headed toward Magnolia Christian Church. This had been a long, trying day. As much as she loved her job, watching those tiny infants fight so hard to live always got to her. She knew she was blessed to have a healthy little boy. And she was also blessed to have such a great after-school program in which to leave that little boy. Jennifer was a wonder with children and Brandon loved seeing his friends after school, even if they did have to finish their homework before they were allowed to play together.

She pulled into the parking lot of the old church. The castle-like building always brought Kate peace. She thought about Parker and prayed he would soon find that same kind of peace for himself. In college, she and Parker had often talked about God. But while Parker believed, he had never practiced any form of religion. Did he pray out there in that big, rambling mansion? Did he see that God gave all good gifts, including his own talent?

She had to admit, she enjoyed seeing Parker, talking to him, getting to know him all over again. This time, things would be different for them. This time, she was older and wiser and more sure of what was important in life. No rushing ahead without thinking, no letting tomorrow take care of itself. This time, she'd take things slowly and enjoy each day, so she could be very, very sure. She had to think of Brandon, of course. And she didn't want to hurt Parker, ever.

She smiled, touched a hand to her lips remembering how Parker had kissed her. It had felt so good and right, it frightened her. Were they rushing things? Did they need more time?

"We have time," Kate said, brushing a hand over her hair. "We've had ten long years to think about it, at least."

But that kiss had erased everything that had kept them apart. Kate knew she was beginning to have deep feelings for Parker. "Just be still and know that He is God," she told herself as she got out of her car.

"Hello there, young lady!"

Turning, Kate smiled at Reverend Rogers. "Hi, Rev. How you doing today?"

The burly minister greeted her with a wave of his meaty hand. "Me, I'm just great. You, however, I am seriously worried about."

Wondering if the good reverend had heard rumors about her and Parker, Kate lifted her eyebrows. "What have I done now?"

He chuckled, his fingers working his car keys. "Well, you were talking to yourself earlier when I came around the corner."

Kate laughed at that. "Maybe I was talking to the Lord."

"Oh, well, in that case, don't let me stop you." He patted her on the arm before he got into his own car, his grin full of understanding. Then he rolled down the window and called out, "You know, it must be going around. I saw another woman out here talking to herself today, too. But before I could get to her to find out who she was, she seemed to vanish into thin air. I don't recall knowing her."

Kate watched as he cranked his car and drove away, her heart tapping out a warning. And again, she felt that funny awareness. But, this was her church. This place was safe, a haven from the world, a haven even to strangers. Maybe the woman Reverend Rob had seen needed to be here, same as Kate.

But then again…with her son inside that church, she didn't like the idea of a stranger lurking about. Not right now, at least.

Glancing around, she hurried into the church to find Brandon. To make sure he was safe.

"I had fun at after-school," Brandon said on the way home. "Miss Jennifer let us play games in the gym."

Kate was relieved that she'd found him laughing in one of the large classrooms with Jacob and a few of the other children.

Jennifer had been fine and so had all the children. Nothing to worry about. She was becoming paranoid. She'd even asked Jennifer how her day had been and her friend had smiled as she talked about cleaning up juice spills and soothing scraped knees. Surely Jennifer would have told her if anything were amiss.

"What kind of games?" she asked Brandon now, determined to keep things on a normal keel whenever he was around.

"Duck, duck, goose and Red Rover, Red Rover, come over, come over," he said in a singsong voice. "I can teach 'em to you if you want."

Laughing, she said, "Actually, I played Red Rover

when I was little. Not so sure about duck, duck, goose, however."

"You need more than two for that one," Brandon said, straining over the backseat as he talked. "Maybe Mr. Parker and Daisy and Patch could play with us."

"Good luck keeping Daisy and Patch in the game," she replied. But she wouldn't mind a little game of spin the bottle with Parker, she thought with a smile.

Brandon giggled, then said, "I know. We can play games at my party. I can't wait! Just four more days."

"Are you sure?" Kate teased. Brandon had been marking off the days on her wall calendar in the kitchen.

"Yep. It's gonna be so awesome."

Kate had to agree with that. Parker was "awesome," allowing them the use of his home and garden, working with Kate to make sure everything was perfect, and his kisses weren't bad either. He'd called her the day after their first kiss, probably with the same mixed feelings she'd had.

"How are you?"

"I'm good. Just getting ready to head off to work."

"I won't keep you long. I just wondered, are we okay, you and me?"

"Why wouldn't we be okay?"

His sigh rattled through the phone line. "I kissed you last night."

"Oh, that." She couldn't help her grin. "I'd forgotten."

"Funny." Then silence.

"Parker, I was teasing. I remember, trust me."

"And?"

"And what?"

"And, how do you feel about that?"

She thought about his lips touching hers and let out

her own soft sigh. She'd gone to sleep with the imprint of that kiss in her mind. How could such a sweet, simple gesture bring her such exquisite peace and joy? "I...I enjoyed it. It was nice."

"*Nice*. I'm not so sure that's a compliment."

"Parker, be serious. I'm all right. You didn't scare me away, if that's what you're wondering."

"But you left once before."

"Maybe because you didn't try to stop me."

"Well, I've changed since then."

"I'm counting on it."

"Mom, the light's green."

Her son's shout from the backseat caused Kate to turn red and quickly snap out of her reverie. "Sorry," she said as a car behind her honked.

"Mom, you need to pay attention," Brandon said with a grin. "Do you need a snack and a nap?"

"Yes, I do," Kate said, "and not necessarily in that order."

"Did the hospital babies cry a lot today?"

"The babies were working hard to grow and get strong enough to go home with their mommies and daddies," she told him, remembering the days when he was so tiny she was almost afraid to touch him. "I've just got a lot to think about. I'll be okay." And it was her turn to monitor the alumni Web site. She'd taken over a while back, to give Jennifer a break and to see if she picked up on any messages or e-mails that someone else might have missed, especially since the site seemed to be drawing in long-lost class members. "I just need some quiet time on the computer, okay?"

Brandon's eyes caught hers in the mirror. "I'll read

that new book Grandma bought me. Then I can play quiet games while you work."

"Okay, sweetie," Kate said, pride swelling inside her heart. Her son was so precious, so loved. She wanted him to know that always. She loved him and God loved him.

She realized she wanted Parker to know that, too. Somehow. Maybe she could convince him to attend church with Brandon and her next Sunday. Just to test the waters, she told herself as she parked the van.

Parker stirred the cream into his coffee, then he opened the back door. The dogs were barking again.

"What is up with you two lately?" he said as he walked out onto the long back porch. Maybe spring was bringing out all the nocturnal creatures. Daisy and Patch seemed to be more high-strung than ever.

But then, so was he.

Kate was back in his life. He still couldn't believe it. She'd come looking for him this time, and she acted as if she actually wanted to *be* in his life, not just supporting him from the sidelines. It didn't make any sense, but who was he to question this turn of events? And who was he to question how he felt, or how she felt for that matter? Thinking about Kate and Brandon gave Parker a new sense of purpose, a reason to come out of his shell and actually live his life for a change.

"Just don't blow it," he told himself as he strolled around the pool, then whistled for the dogs to come in for the night.

The wind picked up, shifting the shadows into dancers moving around the mushrooming, moss-draped live oaks beyond the flagstone deck. A rainstorm was coming, probably one of those long, heavy seasonal storms that would cause everything to turn baby-green and fresh for spring. He saw the lightning shoot like a laser across the sky, then heard the rumble of angry thunder off toward the west. Maybe that was why the dogs were on high alert.

"C'mon, boy," he called to Patch, urging the big dog to come back inside. "It's about to rain."

Daisy followed, hurrying toward him with low growls of greeting. And that's when he saw it. Just a sparkle there around the dog's neck. A chain of some sort, with a round pendant dangling from it.

"Where'd you get this?" Parker asked as he leaned over to stroke Daisy's back. "How in the world—"

It looked like a cheap woman's necklace, something you might win at a carnival or buy at a mall boutique. "Daisy, darlin', when did you decide to wear jewelry?"

Parker held the dog steady as he slipped the long, golden chain off her neck. Then he motioned for both dogs to come inside. Shutting the French doors with a bang, he looked out toward the darkness, wondering how anyone could have gotten close enough to his dogs to put a chain around Daisy's neck. They would have had to have been right up against the fence, and it could have been someone the dogs already knew.

"Let's see what you've got there," he told Daisy, his mind reeling and racing. Then he went to the desk and centered the gaudy pendant underneath the bright light so he could see the picture inside the tiny jeweled frame.

It was Kate's face—taken from their college pictures. Kate's smiling, pretty face.

With the initials *PB* and a harsh, slashing X carved in jagged cuts across the whole thing.

Parker threw the necklace down, then clutched the chair in front of him, shock reverberating throughout his system with the same intensity as the lightning slashing through the night. Then he picked up the phone to call Kate, praying that he'd find her safe and sound.

NINE

Wincing as another round of thunder shook her tiny house, Kate hurried to answer the phone. It was late and she didn't want Brandon to wake up. Between the storm and his birthday excitement she'd never get him back to sleep. "Hello?"

"Thank goodness you're there."

"Parker?" He sounded winded. "Is everything all right?"

"Yes. No. I mean, I was just worried about you and Brandon."

Kate took the cordless phone to the couch, clutching it as she sat down. Outside the wind and rain plummeted and pounded against the windows as the storm intensified.

"Oh, you mean because of the weather? Why are you worried? We're fine. Brandon's all tucked in and I'm just trying to sit through this thunder and lightning. What's wrong?"

He didn't speak for a minute, but she could hear his rushed breathing. "I…something strange happened tonight. The dogs were outside barking. I called them in just before the storm hit, and Daisy was wearing a necklace."

"A necklace?" Frowning, Kate shifted on the couch to tuck her feet underneath her. "What kind of necklace?"

"A locket, sort of. It was a cheap plastic thing, like a miniature picture-frame." He hesitated, then let out another rush of breath. "And it had your college picture in it."

Kate's heart bumped into overdrive. "My picture… That is strange."

"But that's not the only weird part," he said, his tone going low, his next words almost in a whisper. "Your picture had been slashed through with the initials *PB*."

Shocked, Kate sat straight up. "Did you call the police?"

"Not yet. I wanted to make sure you were safe first. And besides, I'm not sure I should call them and say, by the way, my dog is wearing a strange necklace. What would they think?"

The police had been very thorough in questioning each of them at one time or another since the discovery of Josie's skeleton. Everyone was under suspicion. And Parker had purposely avoided any kind of extra attention. If he went to the police with this, they and the media would be all over his estate, looking for clues or, possibly, evidence.

"What should we do?" she asked, trying to stay sane.

The old questions regarding Parker's quirky habits and his need for privacy surfaced in her mind. Was someone trying to scare Parker or warn her? But then, if someone wanted to warn her, that person could just call her or leave her a message. Not put a necklace on one of Parker's dogs. None of this made sense.

Parker's voice came back over the phone wire. "I'll go to the police after Brandon's party. It can wait one more day, and I don't want anything to spoil his birthday. I think they should know that someone did this—I think to threaten me or scare me somehow. And in the meantime, I'm calling my security company to beef up my system. Plus, I'm sending them to install one in your house."

"No," Kate said, throwing a pillow across the couch. "Parker, I have security lights and I installed new stronger locks when I first moved in. I have to be careful because of my work. We get a lot of distraught family members in the neonatal unit, so we're always escorted to our cars by a security guard. And I've lived by myself for a while now. I don't—"

"Kate, someone out there has threatened and stalked all of your friends, and now I think that same person is bringing things around to you and me. It might get very ugly and very dangerous before it's all over. I can't rest while I'm worrying about you and Brandon. Either let me do this for you, or I'm moving you both in here with me."

She heard the concern in his voice, and while it touched her, it also caused a whole new set of worries in her mind.

Parker was beginning to care about Brandon and her, in much the same way she was beginning to have strong feelings about him. But until all of this was over and this terrible crime had been solved, how could they possibly think about a future together?

His voice echoed over the rain and wind. "Are you all right?"

"I'm okay. I don't think I need an alarm system and I can't move in with you, but I promise I'll make sure everything is secure here and I'll think about upgrading the system I have in place. But you have to promise me you'll show the police the necklace as soon as Brandon's party is over on Saturday afternoon."

"I will. I don't like this, Kate. Somebody is deliberately targeting me, and whoever it is knows we've been seeing each other lately. Whoever this is will be after you soon."

Kate's nerves tingled with fear. "So that means we're being watched." And nurses had very structured habits, easy for someone to monitor and follow.

"Yes, I think so. It also means someone got close enough to my estate to get friendly with my dogs. They have the run of the property and some of the fence lines run parallel to the highway—"

"Yes, I found that out the day I tried to get inside," she replied, shaking her head. "It would be easy for someone to reach through the fence with a treat and bribe the dogs."

"I think that's exactly what happened. But I'm going to make sure it doesn't happen again."

Kate heard the anger in his voice. She thought about telling him how she'd been feeling lately, on edge and watchful herself. But that was normal with her high-stress job, and she didn't want to add to his worries. And besides, she had no proof that someone was watching her or even following her.

Instead, she said, "I haven't seen anything out of the ordinary around here, or on the alumni Web site for that matter. But I'll be even more alert if I get any odd messages there."

"You're monitoring the Web site now?"

Hearing the solid concern in his question, she quickly reassured him. "It's okay. I'm just giving Jennifer and the others a break by moderating the blogs and the chat rooms we've set up."

"But do people know you're the moderator now?"

"They know my e-mail name," she said. "You don't think that has something to do with this, do you?"

"It makes sense to me. If someone is watching us, they know we've been together a lot lately and they probably know you're taking care of the Web site, and they might even have access to Lauren's missing laptop. It could be anyone around here who's heard us talking in public—or in private, for that matter."

That realization made her shiver even more, and only reinforced her gut instincts. "Maybe we should go ahead and call the police."

"No, I don't want to ruin Brandon's party. The police and media would swarm my estate. It'll hold for a day or so. But I will take extra measures, starting right now. I'm going to call the security company tonight. At least they can send a guard to cruise your street. That would make me feel better."

"Okay." Kate pushed a hand through her hair. "I don't like this."

"We'll figure it out together," he said. "Now give me a minute to put in that call. I'm going to put you on hold, but don't go away, okay?"

"I'm not going anywhere," Kate replied. "Except to check the locks on the doors and windows."

"Good idea. Hold on."

Kate waited, the phone like a lifeline in her hand as she walked the perimeter of the house, closing blinds and making sure everything was locked tight. She had a porch light out front and there was a streetlight, too. And the security light from the neighbor's house next door glowed across the backyard, sheets of rain moving through its beam. Except for the wet gloomy night, everything looked normal in her backyard. Brandon's cedar tree house and attached swing set huddled near the giant oak tree, the swings squeaking and swaying back and forth in the gusty wind.

Then she saw it. Hanging from one of the big bolts of the swing set. It looked like a necklace glistening in the lights. Kate gasped, straining to stare out at the shadows. Quickly closing the blinds, she hurried to the computer, then pulled up the Web site to see if any unusual messages were posted there. But nothing appeared any different, just the normal chitchat.

Then she saw a new post.

Does anyone have a clue about the locket? I've heard rumors the police are about to question someone connected to that.

"Are you still there?"

Parker's voice in her ear caused her to jump. "Yes, I'm here." Staring at the computer, she said, "And I think someone is trying to tell us something." Quickly reading him what she saw there on the screen, she added, "I saw something hanging on Brandon's swing set out back. At least I think I did. It looks like a necklace."

"I'm coming over there."

He'd hung up before she could protest. But now that the line was dead between them, Kate had to admit she'd be glad to see Parker.

The phone rang again. "It's me. Stay on the line with me until I get there, okay?"

"Okay." She breathed a relieved sigh.

"A security patrol will be on your street in five minutes."

She could hear him cranking his car. "Wow, I'm impressed. You must have a lot of clout."

"I have a lot of money," he deadpanned. She heard tires squealing.

Just to keep herself sane, she asked, "Bragging, are you?"

"Just telling it like it is. At least I can use it for good instead of evil."

That word sent chills down Kate's spine. "Somebody out there is evil, though. What if Brandon had seen that locket?"

"He won't. I'll get to it before he does."

"How could this happen?"

"I don't know, but Daisy and Patch are going to get a few lessons on being better watchdogs, that's for sure. I've tried to stay out of this whole murder scandal, but it looks like someone wants me involved. I heard the dogs barking, but I thought they were just barking at the wind. They tried to warn me in their own way."

"Who would do this, Parker?"

"I don't know. And we don't even know if the necklace I found has anything to do with that crime. We'll have to compare it with the one in your yard."

"Someone must know about the locket the police found." She hesitated, then added, "Judging by the Web site blog rumors are flying. Someone knows more than they're saying, obviously."

"I don't like this." His voice softened then. "I don't want you and Brandon involved."

Hearing a car motor, Kate looked through the front blind. "The security car is here."

Even then, he refused to hang up. "I'm turning onto your street."

"You drove too fast."

"My car has special handicap powers. It's a go-fast kind of thing."

Kate relished the calm tone of his words. He was trying to make her feel better. And she did, the minute she let him in the door. He kissed her, then walked straight through the house. "You stay here. I'm going to get that necklace."

Kate waited at the back door, praying whoever left the necklace wasn't still out there. Parker lifted the necklace off the bolt and hurried back through the muddy yard. Once he was back inside, he held it up to Kate. "It's exactly like the one I found."

Kate stared down at the plastic miniature frame, her hand going to her mouth as she saw her own picture there. And the initials PB with the jagged marks across the entire thing.

"Sit down," Parker said, guiding her to a chair. He got her a glass of water, then sat down beside her. "Now we have to show this to the police, too."

Kate eyed the cheap, garish necklace. "I know. But I think you're right that we should wait—the party's Saturday. I'd hate to ruin that now."

Parker took her hand. "Agreed. We wait until after the party, then we both go to the police and tell them about this. Until then, I'm going to spend as much time as I can with you and Brandon."

"I have to work tomorrow and Brandon has school and after-school activities at the church day care—both with good security," she said, looking over at him.

"We need to alert the school and Jennifer at day care."

"I will." She didn't want to be so afraid, but this was serious. "I'll just tell them to watch out. The police might not take this seriously, but I certainly intend to."

"Which is why I don't want to leave you."

"Let's go into the den," she said, taking his hand. "I couldn't sleep now, anyway. At least the rain has died down."

He pulled away. "First, let's put this in a plastic bag. The rain might have washed off any prints, but it's worth a shot."

Kate got a bag and carefully dropped the necklace inside. Then she turned back to him. "Your initials— someone is certainly trying to scare me."

He grabbed her hand. "Kate, you have to know—"

"I know someone is trying to scare me. That's what I know right now. I don't believe you had anything to do with Josie's murder, Parker. I know that in my heart."

He breathed a long sigh of relief, then tugged her close. "Thank you."

After they'd settled on the couch, he asked, "What do you want to talk about?"

Kate glanced toward where they'd left the necklace on the table. "Anything but this case."

He nodded. "It's hard to put that out of my mind, but for now we can certainly change the subject."

"Well, then, we can't exactly go down memory lane, can we?"

"Let's just concentrate on you and me and the memories we have—the good ones."

She settled back against the couch. "Does that include our most recent memories?"

He let out a chuckle. "Good idea. I like our recent memories a lot."

So they talked about Brandon's winning soccer team and about Parker's latest comic-book creation. He told her he was scheduled to attend a big comic-book convention in Atlanta later in the year. And he told her about all those weeks in the hospital and how his sister Crystal had urged him to draw and write, to take his mind off his pain.

"Then Crystal entered one of my stories in a contest," he explained. "And—"

"And the rest, as they say, is history," Kate finished, pride swelling inside her heart. "Parker, I know your accident was horrible, and you've been through so many surgeries and all the therapy, but I believe things happen for a reason. And I believe you needed that time after your accident to become the man you are today. I think God was working in your life, even then."

He huffed a breath. "So you think God planned for me to be crippled?"

She heard the doubt and scorn in his words. "I believe God has a plan for each of us, and sometimes we have to suffer before that plan comes to light."

"So you marrying Dexter was part of the plan?"

"Maybe. I had to learn not to be so impatient and impulsive, that's for sure. But I don't regret marrying Dexter, because it gave me Brandon."

"You sure see things in a different light than I do," he countered. But he didn't sound as cynical and bitter as he had in the past. "I guess I'd never thought about things in that way. I did question God though. It's kind of ironic that I never asked for His help, but I sure questioned Him a lot. And blamed Him, too. I blamed Him for my mother's death and for my accident. And I've blamed Him for a very long time, because, well, it seems He's left me all alone."

Kate's heart melted at his admission. "It must have been hard, losing first your father, and then later your mother when you were still so young."

"It was," he replied. "But Crystal is a good older sister. She took care of both of us. At least I can pay her back now and help her out with her own kids." Then he chuckled. "So tell me, how can I pay God back—I mean for bringing you back into my life."

"You have to put God *into* your way of thinking," she said, the glow of his words giving her courage. "That's how I cope, good or bad. We can't blame God for all the bad things in our life, if we've never turned to Him and thanked Him for all the good things that happen." Then she lowered her voice, her fingers brushing over the chenille throw she kept on the couch. "Parker, all that time you thought you were alone—well, you weren't. God was there. You just forgot that He was."

He was silent for a long time. Then he said, "Well, I'm thinking about Him now, and I'm thanking Him, really thanking Him. You amaze me."

Kate felt a rich warmth moving throughout her insides. Had she reached him? Had she found that dark, lonely place inside Parker's soul and filled it with a little bit of hope and light? "I just want you to understand why my faith is so important to me."

"I'm beginning to understand a lot of things," he said.

She didn't need him to explain. They'd known each other for years in college. But now, they were working toward knowing each other for life. That made things a lot more intimate between them.

And Kate treasured their newfound intimacy.

Even if she still had those niggling doubts in the back of her mind. She'd just have to do as she'd told Parker: she'd turn to God and let Him show her the way.

After checking her yards and making sure the security patrol would stay all night, Parker had left around midnight. Now he turned out the light and lay in the darkness, the dogs curled up nearby in their plush bed on the floor.

The rain was falling soft and steady outside his second-floor bedroom. He could see the reflection of the bright drops in the security lights just beyond the French doors. He wasn't worried for his own safety. He had a top-of-the-line security system and the dogs knew to be on alert when the house settled for the night.

But he was worried about Kate and Brandon. Which is why he'd instructed the security company to put a patrol on her street around the clock.

Whoever you are, you have my attention now, he thought.

But who? And why?

He thought about Josie, back to their brief time as friends in college. Josie had been a lot like him, an outsider. Quiet, shy, plain by most standards. But she'd had a sweet smile and a wry sense of humor, whenever anyone took the time to get to know her. Parker had considered Josie a friend, but nothing more. Not like Kate.

Now he wondered what secrets Josie had carried around with her all those years ago. Why on earth would anyone kill Josie? And had someone decided that he, Parker, knew about the murder? He lay there racking his brain for clues, trying to remember conversations he'd had with Josie. When was the last time he'd seen her?

Then he remembered.

It had been the night of his accident. Josie had been sitting alone in a booth in Burt's Pizza. Parker had waved to her, but didn't stop to talk. He'd been in a hurry that night. He had flowers in the car and Kate's favorite—mushroom pizza—on order. After picking it up, he'd planned on going to see Kate and asking her for a date. Their first real date.

He sat up in bed, pushing a hand through his hair. He remembered waving to Josie. But they hadn't actually talked that night.

Had she been crying?

He couldn't remember. But he did remember that she'd looked all alone and sad. And he hadn't even bothered to go check on her. "Some friend you are," he whispered in the darkness.

No, that wasn't the very last time—she had come to visit him in the hospital after the accident. He was so groggy from the painkillers, he couldn't remember much. But she had looked like she was crying. He assumed at the time because she was worried about him. He got up to limp over to the French doors.

The rain-soaked yard beyond the columned, wrap-around porch was dark and drenched in shadows, the moss-covered live oaks hovering like hunchbacked giants in the night. He stared out toward the gate, making sure it was well-lit and secure. The road was quiet and deserted, or at least he hoped it was.

Could someone be out there watching him even now?

Parker's whole being ached with longing, a need that had been building since the night he'd seen Kate again at the reunion. He didn't like being alone anymore. And it had nothing to do with fear of who might be out there in the shadows.

It had everything to do with what now lay open and bare in his own soul. He didn't want to be alone anymore. He wanted to be with Kate and her son.

And so he closed his eyes and prayed. And he realized that right now, standing here in the dark, he was not alone.

God was there. And thanks to Kate, Parker was ready to acknowledge that, at long last. And this time, he would do so publicly because it no longer mattered who else saw him or judged him, or even tried to scare him off. He was in this with Kate now, and he intended to protect her and keep her safe, so that he could have a life, a real life, with her and Brandon.

"They're all messing up my life!"

She slammed the door of the cheap motel room with a bang, then threw her scarf and gloves down. Her plans to leave Kate Brooks a little gift had almost been thwarted by the storm. But she had managed to leave her gift in the backyard and put a hint or two on that stupid Web site. Surely Kate would see that. And surely Parker would have found his matching gift by now. And as for the rest…

"I'll do it soon," she decided, her boot heels clicking on the matted motel carpet as she stripped out of her wet raincoat.

She smiled at herself in the mirror. She hoped the

plastic lockets had both of them stewing and sweating, especially Parker. This had all started with Parker anyway. And maybe it would all end with him. The man obviously had a great deal of money. And he had a very soft spot. No, make that two very soft spots.

Kate Brooks and her brat of a son, Brandon.

What would Parker pay to protect both of them? She'd have to test the waters to find out. If her plan worked, she would be able to get out of this town for good. And no one would ever know the truth. And, even better, Parker Buchanan would get what he deserved, at last.

TEN

"What a perfect day for a party!"

Grace rubbed her hands together with such glee, Kate thought her mother would surely crack her twinkling diamond rings.

"It *is* a nice day," Kate said, all of her recent late-night worries gone in the glow of a warm spring sun. In spite of her uneasiness about finding that strange locket in her yard, she intended to get through this party for her son's sake. She'd considered canceling the whole thing, but Brandon would have been devastated. And besides, if they canceled, that would only bring up more questions about Parker. They'd go to the police immediately after the party and then together they could explain that someone seemed to be targeting Parker. Until then, she'd just have to put on a happy face for her son. And her mother. "I'm glad that storm the other night didn't do too much damage."

Grace glanced around Parker's backyard. "Well, if it did, I think our Mr. Buchanan must have hired an entire team to clean up the debris. This garden is stunning."

High praise, coming from her persnickety mother, Kate thought with a smile. But she agreed. Parker had outdone himself over the past two days. The storm had brought out the first dogwood blossoms of spring and opened up the rest of the camellias and azaleas, and Parker had turned the entire yard into a carnival for children.

In one corner, a space walk shaped like a castle was up and running. On the other side of the sloping grounds past the pool, a tent was set up, complete with face painters, clowns, arcade games, a hotdog and hamburger vendor and even a portable pizza oven. And underneath the tent, bright tables and chairs in primary colors were set up to match the bright red-and-white awning and the blues and greens of the castle. Balloons of the same colors billowed all around the property, even at the open front gate where a security guard was checking off the names of the hired help and the invited guests.

Refusing to think about the implications of having such tight security, Kate instead watched her son. This day was for Brandon. She wouldn't ruin it with thoughts of what might lie just beyond those gates.

"Look at all the Patchman stuff," Brandon said as he rushed by with some of his friends, all of them squealing with delight at every turn.

Parker had ordered several life-size versions of Patchman and his cohorts and had placed them at various locations all around the yard.

"I see, I see," Kate called after her son, twirling around just in time to look up toward the porch where Parker stood watching, a soft smile covering his face.

"I honestly think the man is smitten," Grace said as she leaned close, her eyebrows arching as she indicated Parker with a lift of her chin. "And I have to say, I've never seen you so happy."

"I *am* happy," Kate replied.

She hadn't told her mother about the strange lockets that they'd found. And she surely wasn't going to mention to Grace that her tiny house now had twenty-four-hour security. Or that she had insisted the security company send her the bill, even after they informed her that it had already been taken care of by Mr. Buchanan. But she meant to talk to Parker about that, and all of this, too.

A clown with a drooping, sad face danced by then spun around to hand Kate a bright yellow-and-white plastic flower.

Kate took the flower, thinking she'd never really liked clowns. And this one looked downright depressing with that upside-down pouting expression.

"Honey, is everything all right?" Grace asked now, her question full of a mother's intense scrutiny.

Kate dropped the gaudy flower onto a nearby table. "Fine, Mother. I just…I hope I didn't let things get too out of hand."

"You mean with the party, or the man standing on the porch?"

"Both," Kate admitted, her hands on her hips. "I have to speak to Parker about a few things."

"Well, I imagine so," Grace replied with a tart smile. "Go ahead. I think if you don't get up on that porch this minute, that man is going to swoop down here and steal you away."

"You are way too dramatic," Kate said, but she could feel Parker's gaze following her as she strolled across the yard, her blue linen sundress billowing out around her.

Pulling her lightweight matching sweater close, she hurried up the steps. "Everything is perfect, Parker. I never expected this much, though."

His gaze washed over her, warming her much more than the sun. "I'm glad you like it."

"I do. And Brandon is thrilled. But this is too much. How can I ever pay you back?"

He frowned, then leaned against his black Patchman cane. "I don't expect you to do that. This is my gift to Brandon, for his birthday."

"But this…and the security guard." She pulled her hair away from her face. "I'm used to taking care of myself. I don't let my mother pay my bills and I don't expect you to start doing that, either."

He looked confused and then hurt. "I'm sorry. I never thought—I didn't mean to imply that you couldn't afford the party or the security, Kate. I wanted to do this, for you and Brandon."

"I know you did, and it's so sweet, and Brandon likes you so much, but—"

He touched a finger to her wrist. "But you're afraid he'll get too attached to me and maybe expect too many material things?"

"Yes," she said, bobbing her head. "I've tried not to spoil him, and I won't let Mother and Judge Duncan spoil him, but of course, we do just a little bit. But he looks up to you so much and he sees all that you have to offer, and not just material things, but you've been a real role model to him. I don't want him to be disappointed."

He glanced away, then looked straight at her. "And *you* don't want to be disappointed, either, right?"

"I didn't say that."

"Do I disappoint you?"

She looked into his eyes and saw the pain he'd tried to hide for so long. "You have never been a disappointment to me. You were always a good friend, even when I probably didn't deserve you. And now, well, now I think of you as much more than just a friend. But I don't want you to spoil me either. I can take care of myself."

"But what if I *want* to take care of you? Would that be so wrong?"

She couldn't deny that being around him made her feel cherished and safe. "No, that's not so wrong. Just don't shower me with any more expensive gifts, okay."

"I've bought you pizza, given you lilies and hired a guard to protect your home. Not exactly diamonds and roses."

"I don't need diamonds and roses," she said. Then she smiled, hoping to lighten the mood. "But I sure do love the lilies." Then she pointed to a nearby bush. "And your camellias."

"They're yours," he replied, a twinkle in his eyes.

She held up a hand. "Don't go sending me a team of gardeners with truckloads of camellias, okay?"

He reached out to a bush near the steps and plucked a bright blushing-pink variegated flower. "How about one perfect blossom?"

Kate took the fluffy flower and held it close. "This is exactly what I needed today."

Parker smiled at her, relief clear on his face. "It's been a tough week. Let's just give Brandon this day and then we'll take the lockets to the police and see what happens next."

She nodded, then moved to turn away.

"Kate?" His hand on her arm held her there.

"What?"

He pulled her close for a quick hug. "It's going to be all right, I promise."

She stepped back to gaze into his eyes. "I know."

Then he let her go, but stood close. "And you and Brandon are exactly what *I* needed today. You've brought me back to life."

Kate couldn't hide the tears misting in her eyes. Afraid of the feelings washing over her as she looked up at him, she could only nod and smile as she turned to go back out into the yard.

At the table where Kate had dropped the big plastic flower, the sad clown stood looking toward the house. Kate watched as the clown picked up the discarded flower, then turn with an embellished huff back toward the waiting children.

"Guess I offended him," Kate thought, smiling to herself. Well, she didn't need the clown's fake flower. She had a real blossom from Parker. And she would cherish it forever.

The party was soon in full swing, causing Kate to forget all the nagging uneasiness of the past week. The children were having a great time, while she basked in the warmth of Parker's attention. There was so much more she wanted to say to him, to explain to him. But that would have to wait until they could be alone later.

Thankfully, there had been no more cryptic comments on the Web site and neither of them had received any more strange surprises. The beefed-up security seemed to be helping, but even today, in the

midst of all of the lighthearted fun, the signs that something was amiss couldn't be denied. Especially when all
of her friends still doubted Parker.

Kate stood in Parker's massive kitchen now,
chatting away with the potluck group, one eye on the
kids her mother and some of the other parents were
supervising outside and the other ever aware of Parker
out there having as much fun as the little children.
Daisy and Patch danced in circles around all the guests,
eager to have so many willing participants to help them
play fetch.

"I've never seen Parker Buchanan so animated,"
Cassie said, nudging Kate in the ribs. "You've certainly
brought him around."

Kate dipped her head to hide her goofy smile. "More
like he's just coming out of his shell."

"Tell me," Jennifer chimed in. "All these years he's
been back and no one around here has even been invited
inside this amazing house, not to mention we never see
him anywhere around town." She playfully patted Kate
on the back. "Whatever you're doing, keep at it. Parker
brings a lot of prestige to the community. And I like that
smile you're trying so hard to hide."

Dee didn't look so sure. "But I still wonder about
why he's been so reclusive up until now. Kate?"

Kate didn't like the doubt in her friend's eyes. "He's
just always been a very private person. Even back in
college. But I think now it had a lot to do with his injury.
He's kind of self-conscious about his limp."

"That's understandable," Jennifer said. "But he has
the coolest canes. I think he looks very debonair, even
if I don't quite trust the man."

Kate had to agree on the first point, but she defended Parker on the second. "The man looks good, I can't deny that. And I *do* trust him."

"Well, I love his kitchen, that's for sure." Lauren pulled more cookies out of the oven. "Okay, this batch is good to go." Placing them on the counter to cool, she leaned close. "So, Kate, what's the scoop? Just how serious are things between you and Parker?"

Kate stood looking from one friend to the other. How could she explain her feelings for Parker? How could she make her friends see him as she saw him? "Things are progressing," she said, careful to keep her voice low. "Parker is a good man." She waved her hands in the air. "But then, I don't have to show y'all that. Look what he did for Brandon."

"Very nice of him," Steff said, rolling her eyes. "Do you think maybe he did this for you? I mean—to impress you?"

Kate glanced toward Steff, standing by the open French doors, watching Trevor's two young nephews learning how to juggle with one of the clowns who'd been hired for the party. "What is that supposed to mean?"

Steff pushed away from the door. "Oh, I don't know. I guess I just remember that Parker always had a crush on you. We all knew it. And now, well, he's rich, single and very available. He might be trying to buy your love."

Kate frowned at that notion. "It never entered my mind." Then she remembered her conversation with Parker earlier. Touching the camellia Grace had pinned to her daughter's sweater, she shook her head. "Parker knows how I feel about that. I mean, I fussed at him for going overboard with this party—"

"But you're enjoying it, right?" Cassie asked, her green eyes bright with mirth. "Who wouldn't?"

"I'm not letting all of this go to my head," Kate countered. "Parker and I have both agreed that we can't move forward until this pall hanging over everyone is gone."

Lauren nodded as the room went silent. "You mean, the murder case, of course?"

"Of course," Kate replied, her efforts to keep that subject at bay disappearing like a runaway helium balloon. "All of us are in danger, whether we want to believe it or not. Look at everything that this case has brought to the surface. Look at what we have all gone through. The more we become involved, the more dangerous it becomes." Stopping short of telling them about her own scare, she heaved a breath.

Lifting a hand toward Cassie, she sent her friend some sympathy. "Cassie lost her brother, Scott, and we still don't know who is to blame. Even Cornell Rutherford can't be trusted anymore. All we know for sure right now is that someone is out there trying to terrorize all of us, and we can't hide that with balloons and birthday cake. How can I even think about a future with Parker when I don't feel safe in my own home?"

She stopped, realizing all of her friends were passing each other concerned looks. "I'm sorry. I've just been so busy lately and I'm worried—"

"Did something happen on the Web site?" Jen asked, her hand on Kate's arm. "Are you being threatened?"

Kate looked down at the counter, hating that she was going to withhold information from her friends. "No, just a few new e-mails here and there, but nothing I can put a finger on. I'm just jittery. I'll be okay. I keep going over and over everything that's happened and I can't get it out of my mind. I just need answers. We all need answers."

She wanted to tell them the whole story, but that would just set all of them off against Parker again. How could she even begin to explain the lockets and the implications of those initials? They'd all immediately assume Parker was hiding something. If they didn't already.

Dee took a sip of soda, then cleared her throat. "Parker was good friends with Josie Skerritt. And he certainly would have it in for Penny. The wreck was her fault."

Kate saw it in their eyes. They did suspect Parker. "We all knew Josie and Penny," she reminded them. "And we still don't know where Penny is. Besides, Parker liked Josie, and he hasn't seen Penny since college."

"None of us have," Jennifer reminded her, the implications of that statement floating through the air.

Dee didn't back off either. "Have you asked Parker about his past with Josie?"

"They didn't have a past," Kate retorted. "They were just friends. That's all I need to know."

"Maybe that's all Parker wants you to know," Lauren replied. "And maybe that's why you're so on edge today."

Kate couldn't believe how they were turning on Parker, and standing right here in his kitchen while they did it. "Look, I trust Parker. I *know* him. I refuse to believe he's hiding anything from us. Parker wouldn't do that to me."

"Thanks for the vote of confidence."

They all looked up to find Parker standing at the open doors of the kitchen, his expression grim, shocked. And relentless in its anger.

ELEVEN

The room suddenly became very quiet. The sound of children's cheerful laughter bounced off the tense atmosphere inside the big kitchen. Parker felt like a condemned man meeting his jurors.

Kate glanced from Parker back to her friends. "I'm sorry," she said. "I guess everyone's a bit wired these days. We were just discussing all the speculation."

"And *me*," he added as he stepped farther into the kitchen. "You were all discussing me." Then his gaze moved over the women standing around the work island. Trying to hide the uneasy feeling inside his heart, he asked, "What do you want to know, ladies?"

Steff looked guilty, her eyes filling with resolve. "Parker, we didn't mean to imply—"

"Yes, you did." He walked to the counter before he responded. "And I guess I can't blame you. I haven't been very forthcoming over the years. But I'm not going to try to defend myself. I have no reason to do so."

Cassie glanced toward Lauren and Steff. "Let's just go back out to the party and pass out these cookies."

"Good idea," Jennifer said, pushing toward the door. "Parker—"

"Go on," he said, moving out of her way. "I'd like to talk to Kate anyway." Then he added, "Alone, if y'all aren't afraid to leave her with me, that is."

The other women scattered like a flock of pretty birds, leaving Kate standing across the counter from him. He searched her face, looking for the same signs of doubt he'd seen in her friends' eyes. "Do you really trust me?" he asked, needing to hear it now that it was just the two of them.

"You know I do," she replied, coming around the counter to touch a hand to his arm. "Parker, they're just worried and we're all a bit frazzled these days. Things keep going from bad to worse and no one can explain who's behind all of this. I didn't tell them about the lockets, either. And I guess I feel bad about holding back that information."

"Or you didn't tell them because you think they'd automatically accuse me of something."

"Why would you send yourself or me a fake locket?"

He looked down at the counter. "I could have bought that locket and then planted the same type of locket on your property—or at least that's what they'd assume."

"But you didn't. I believe in you, Parker. I do."

He thought maybe she was just trying to convince herself, but he let that ride for now. "But your friends think that it might be me."

"They're just trying to rationalize all of this. Please don't hold it against them."

He pushed further. "But they don't seem to have a problem holding the past against me. Look, Kate, I never did fit in with that crowd and I still don't. I won't have them badgering you just because you're with me."

"I don't care about that," she said, her eyes wide. "Parker, this is me, remember? This is Kate. Have I ever treated you as if you don't fit in?"

He shook his head. "No. You've always been kind to me. But don't confuse kindness with putting yourself out on a limb. And don't confuse pity for real feelings."

"Oh, please," she said, her tone huffy as she hit a hand against the counter. "I'm not that nice, trust me. And I can't see any reason to pity someone who's successful, honorable and willing to go out on a limb for my child and me. I care about you, but you seem too dense to believe it."

A surprised smile slipped across his lips. "Well, I am dense, that's for sure. I just don't want to hurt you, Kate."

"Then stop being so down on yourself." She came closer then, taking his hands in hers. "Parker, you said something to me earlier that's hard to forget. You said Brandon and I were exactly what you needed today. And I believe that with all my heart. You *needed* to do this—throw this party, help me—more than we needed you to do all of it. I can see that now. I understand that. We all need a purpose, a reason to live. My faith has taught me that. My purpose is my son, and helping babies to survive and grow strong. Your talent has helped you with your purpose. Through your work, you give kids a solid understanding of how to do the right things, make the right choices in life. But you've been out there winging it for so long, you've forgotten the source of all that talent."

He stared down at her, all of his deeply embedded doubts rising to the surface like leaves floating on water. "You mean God?"

"Yes," she said, her eyes misty. "I mean Christ. Parker, think about all of our talks. About how we were separated for a reason. And now, here we are after so many years, back together. We have a second chance. I believe that with all my heart. I believe we can help each other. I believe in you."

Parker heaved a breath as he pulled her close, his hands pushing through her hair as he leaned down to kiss her. He wanted to believe her, he wanted to trust God. But she was right; he'd been on his own for so long, he didn't know how to take that next step. He backed away, turning to clutch the counter. "What if I do begin to trust God, Kate? What if I give myself over to Him and still get hurt? I don't think I could take that."

He heard her long sigh. "I can't promise that won't happen. But I can tell you this. We need God in our lives through the good and the bad. He rejoices with us through the good times, and He suffers with us through all the bad. But as long as we keep Him close, Parker, we can get through anything. He gives us that kind of strength."

"Together?" he said, turning back to face her. "You believe we can get through anything together, and with God's help?"

"Yes," she said, rushing into his arms. "Yes. He *will* help us cope, He *will* shield us from all those doubters, but it won't always be easy. I believe we can make it, with God's guidance. And even if the worst happens, and whoever this is tries to do us harm, I know somehow we'll find a way, because we have each other now. We have each other and our faith."

Parker pulled her close again, then closed his eyes, scared by her soft intensity. "Kate, you don't know how much that means to me. You can't understand what you've done for me."

She lifted her head. "Yes, I do, Parker. And I feel the same way. You've done a lot for me, too. And Brandon. It means so much to me, being here with you."

He kissed her again, the sound of children laughing adding to the joy that seemed to be pressing against all the walls he'd built up around himself. That joy wanted to burst through, but he was afraid to open his heart completely—until he could come to her free and clear, with no secrets and no doubts.

"I need you," he told her, his words whispered against the sweet scent of her hair. "But first, we need to help the others find this killer. That has to be our purpose right now."

Kate touched a hand to his face. "You're right. But I just need to know I can count on you."

"You can," he said. "Don't ever doubt that."

He was about to kiss her again when the doorbell rang. Giving her a reluctant look, he said, "We seem to have a late arrival."

Kate pulled away. "Want me to answer it?"

"C'mon," he said. "Let's go together, then we'll tell Brandon it's time to open his presents."

She took his hand as they crossed the kitchen to the entry hall, her smile soft and secure.

But Kate's smile died on her lips when Parker opened the door to find police investigators Nikki Rivers and Jim Anderson standing on his front porch.

And neither one of them was smiling.

* * *

Nikki Rivers pushed at her long ponytail, then gave Parker an unflinching stare. "Mr. Buchanan, you need to come down to the station with us."

Parker looked from the two officers standing at the front door of his house to the woman standing in shock behind him. Before he could speak, Kate pushed her way around him.

"What are you talking about?" she asked, glaring at the investigators, daring either of them to step forward.

Out in the backyard, the birthday party was in full swing and Parker didn't want this to ruin Brandon's big day. And it sure wouldn't do for Kate's mother or her friends to find out that Parker was being hauled away by the police.

"What do you want?" he asked, his tone firm and in control in spite of the anxiety he felt. He wasn't worried for himself, but he didn't want Kate to have to suffer through this mess.

"We just need to ask you some questions," one of the officers answered.

Parker knew both of them. He'd gone to college with Nikki Rivers and he'd seen her partner, Jim Anderson, around town. He knew why they were here. Hadn't he been expecting this visit? Funny that they'd been talking about this very thing not minutes before, and Kate's friends hadn't tried to hide their doubts regarding Parker. And funny that Kate believed in him, had just declared that to him. He sure hoped God would see them through this, because Parker had a sick feeling that this would be the worst test of his faith yet.

He glanced at Kate, thinking it made sense that their

time together would have to come to an end. Wasn't that just his luck? Whenever something good started happening in his life, the bad was soon to follow.

"Let me get my jacket and cane," Parker said, pulling Kate back away from the door. "Go get the lockets," he whispered.

"I can come with you," she said, her eyes dark with anxiety.

"No, you can't leave Brandon. Just get that plastic bag from your purse."

Turning to the waiting detectives, Kate said, "I'll be right back."

Then Parker limped to a nearby umbrella stand to grab one of his walking sticks. A more sedate one than the whimsical Patchman cane he'd been using for the party. He picked a silver-handled one made from rosewood, his demeanor calm and calculated. He couldn't let this interruption ruin what had just happened between Kate and him.

She came back into the foyer, the plastic bag in her hand. "Here, Parker."

Taking her aside, he said, "I'll just go and get this over with soon." Trying to reassure her, he added, "If I cooperate, I should be back before all the cake is gone."

"They can't do this," Kate said, turning toward him, her blue eyes full of doubt and fear. "Parker, you should call Seth, at least. You might need a lawyer."

"I don't have anything to hide," he replied, memories swirling like ink spots in front of his eyes. "Look, Josie knew all of us. It's only natural they'd want to question me, especially since she and I were good friends." He shrugged, gave her a warning look, then glanced toward the officers. "I'm surprised they haven't already called me. And I do have something that might interest them, remember?" He held up the bag.

Nikki glanced to her partner, then back to Parker. "What's that? Birthday cake for the boys down at the station?"

Parker shot her a grim look. "This is something Kate and I had planned on bringing to you after her son's birthday party."

Kate stood back, her hands at her sides. She turned toward Nikki. "Can't you just talk to us both here? C'mon inside where we can talk privately and I'll make some coffee."

Nikki shook her head then looked down at the planked porch floor. "Sorry, we can't do that, Kate. We've been ordered to bring him in—just for questioning."

"And we can't go into the details," Jim said, his tone apologetic. Then he looked back at Parker. "It shouldn't take too long."

Parker nodded, then tugged on his jacket. "I'll be back soon," he told Kate, hoping that was the truth. "Just stay here and keep the party going. Wait for me, okay?"

Kate gave a quick nod. "I'll be right here, I promise. But what should I tell Brandon?" she asked, her blue eyes widening. "He's going to wonder why you're not out there with everyone?"

Parker leaned close, taking in the floral scent of her perfume. Wrapping his arms around her, he gave her a light hug, then closed his eyes to block out the memories—both the old ones he still held inside his heart and the new ones he'd made with Kate and her son. "Tell him I'm helping the police find the bad guy."

Then he let her go and left with the two officers.

And tried to put the feel of her in his arms out of his mind.

Outside the party continued with kids running through the grass and clowns blowing up balloons. But one lone clown stood to the side and let go of a single yellow balloon, then watched as it floated up into the trees.

TWELVE

Kate stood staring at her sleeping son, her mind in turmoil over Parker being taken away. Why would they want to question Parker, of all people? And why wasn't he back yet?

She'd promised to stay at Magnolia Hall until he got home, but because of the protests from her friends and her mother, Kate hadn't kept that promise. They were all in an uproar over this, of course. They'd managed to keep it from the other parents, telling anyone who'd asked that Parker had been called away on an emergency.

And this *was* an emergency. Parker was being targeted for something he didn't do.

With her mother's help and close scrutiny, Kate had reluctantly closed up the big house, made sure the dogs were fed, then left Parker a note telling him to call her.

So she sat, waiting. She couldn't relax, but at least she'd insisted Brandon needed to rest after his busy day. She'd settled him down in his room, letting him watch some of the new DVDs he'd gotten at the party. When he'd asked about Parker, Kate told her son that Parker would probably see him tomorrow. It hadn't taken long for Brandon to fall asleep with the DVD player still running.

Now, jittery and worried, Kate couldn't stop checking on her son. Brandon sighed, then rolled over. He was probably exhausted. He'd been so excited about this birthday party, and he'd been disappointed that Parker had to leave right in the middle of the festivities. After all the presents had been opened and Kate had run out of excuses, her friends had helped make sure each child received autographed copies of the Patchman comic books and some other goodies as a parting gift. After that, even the clowns had all loaded up and left, too.

But everyone had left with the same question in mind—where was Parker? She hated to think what would be said when the whole town did find out. This wasn't fair to Parker. None of this was.

The phone she'd tucked inside her robe pocket jingled. Kate stepped out into the hall to answer. "Hello?"

"Darlin', I just wanted to check on you and let you know that Thatch is trying to find out what's going on."

"And did he find out anything?" Kate asked, grateful that her mother wasn't being judgmental.

"Unfortunately, no," Grace replied. "The investigators are keeping a very tight lid on this thing. If Thatch can't get any information, then that's that, I'm afraid. Have you heard anything from Parker?"

"No." Kate glanced at the clock. "I'm so worried," she said, staring at the white lilies Parker had given her.

"You and Brandon should have come home with me."

"I'm okay, Mother. And Brandon is asleep. I've got the security patrol right outside."

"I don't like this, not one bit."

"Maybe it'll all be over soon."

"I pray for that to happen," Grace said. "Well, if

you're sure everything is all right, I'm going to go to bed. Although I doubt I'll get very much sleep."

"Thanks, Mother," Kate replied. "I'm going to wait up for Parker."

Grace expelled a sigh. "Just be careful, honey."

After hanging up, Kate couldn't stop thinking of Parker's kisses and the bond they'd shared earlier. She smiled as she thought about the party and how hard they'd all worked to make it special for Brandon. And it *had* been so special, so perfect, up until the time Parker had left with the police.

"Call me," she said out loud, willing the phone to ring. "Parker, please be safe."

She prayed that the police would listen to him and believe him. While it was true Parker and Josie had been close in college, Kate couldn't believe Parker might be her murderer. After having been around Parker and getting to know him better than she'd ever known him in college, Kate knew he would never hurt another living soul. Parker was a good man. He'd been just as shocked as the rest of them to learn the body Trevor had unearthed on the campus was Josie's.

Glancing at her watch, Kate leaned over to tuck Brandon's blanket close around his chest, smiling at his Patchman pajamas. Brandon knew all about the Patchman creed—power, action, trust, compassion and honor. He'd learned all of those traits from the pages of Parker's *Patchman* comic books. And lately, from the man himself. She loved her son so much, and she wanted the best for him. And she had begun to believe Parker Buchanan might just be the best thing for both of them.

Please be safe, Parker, she silently prayed. *Dear God, please help him. Help all of us.*

Then she left Brandon and went into the living room to sit on the couch and wait to hear news from Parker.

And while she waited, she once again pulled out the old, yellowing sketch of herself that Parker had silently handed her as he'd walked by her desk that fall day so long ago.

"I'm not that same girl, Parker," she said, her prayers screaming and silent inside her aching head. "And you're different, too. We have a chance now. We have to get through this."

She couldn't imagine Parker Buchanan a killer.

Getting up, Kate checked the street for the security company car, glad to see it was still there. Then she watched as the night sky grew darker by the minute.

"Parker, where are you?"

Parker found Kate's note the minute he got home. He didn't even stop to look around the house. Instead, he rushed out to his custom-designed sports car and headed straight to Kate's house. She had to know everything that had happened. And she needed to hear it all from him.

As he turned onto her street, he was relieved to see the security patrol out front. And a light on inside the house, too. It wasn't that late, but he'd half expected her to be in bed.

Glad that she was still up, he parked the car, waved to the guard, then grabbed his cane from the seat. Something lying on the passenger's-side floor caught his eye. Frowning, Parker bent over to reach back inside the two-seater, his fingers grasping for the wadded-up piece of paper.

Pulling at the heavy parchment, he inhaled a breath as an old familiar sketch of Kate appeared in the streetlights. It was one of many he'd drawn years ago in college. A close-up of Kate laughing. But this version sent chills down Parker's spine.

Bright-red strokes covered the entire image. And just as with the necklace he'd found, his own initials were scratched across the picture. Scratched across Kate's face.

Then it occurred to Parker that this sick person didn't so much care what the police found out. This person wanted to scare Kate and Parker. Glancing up at the house, Parker felt dread coursing through his body. What if someone had left Kate a similar sketch? What if this person had already been inside Kate's house?

Ignoring the strain on his damaged leg, Parker hurried up the steps and pounded on Kate's door. "Kate, it's me. Let me in."

She opened the door to find him slumped in relief against his cane.

"Parker!" She flew into his arms, almost knocking him back off the small porch.

But Parker managed to balance himself just in time to take her in his arms. "Are you all right?" he asked, his free hand moving over her hair.

"I am now that you're here. Come in and tell me what happened."

Parker followed her inside, the crumpled sketch clutched in one hand. Before he could hide it, Kate grabbed it away from him.

"What's this?"

He watched as her expression changed from curious to shocked, then he dropped his cane and pulled her close. "I found it in my car. Someone is out to hurt both of us, Kate. I think I've been set up to take the fall for Josie Skerritt's murder."

Kate handed Parker a glass of tea, then sat down beside him. "Tell me everything, beginning with how you found that sketch."

He nodded, drank a swallow or two, then pinched his thumb and forefinger against the bridge of his nose. "I found that in my car, just now. Somebody managed to get past all of my security to leave that in my garage."

Kate closed her eyes, then touched at her hair. "During the party today?"

"I don't know. Probably. That makes sense, since so many people were coming and going."

"But we were so careful."

"Apparently not careful enough."

Kate took the sketch into her shaking hands, carefully placing it on the table, then asked, "And what about the police? What did they tell you?"

"They confirmed that the body was Josie's. But then, we knew that."

Kate watched his face, seeing the shadows underneath his eyes. "It's really Josie? I kept hoping they were wrong."

He nodded. "They think I killed her. They think… they said she was pregnant when she died, and Kate, they think I'm the father." He leaned forward, his hands falling against his legs. "And that's not all. The initials on the locket are PB, and there's a picture of a baby inside."

Kate felt her world shifting, as if she'd lost her

balance. She could see everything spinning out of control, could feel the weight of gravity pulling her down. She had to find the strength to fight, to hold on.

She grabbed Parker, her breath heaving as tears formed in her eyes. "Oh, no. No, Parker. No."

Then she glanced up at him, confusion warring with hope inside her soul. "Tell me this isn't true. Please, Parker, you have to tell me this isn't true."

Parker held her tight against him. "It's not true. I didn't kill Josie, and I can't be the father of the baby. Josie and I never…we were never together like that."

He lifted her head, his hand holding her chin. "You have to believe me. I need you to believe me."

Kate tried to nod, tried to put the image of the red slashes on that sketch and the lockets out of her mind. She couldn't breathe, couldn't find her voice.

"You don't believe me, do you?" Parker asked, pushing away from her to stare over at her. "Kate?"

Kate got up to pace around the room, unsure what to do or say. "Parker, are you sure you're telling me everything?"

"Yes," he said, his words weary and hesitant. "I told the police everything I know. I showed them the toy necklaces. Now I have to show them this sketch. And they want to question you."

Kate kept pacing, but he halted her with a hand on her arm. "Kate, someone was inside my house. Someone found this sketch in my office files and did this to it. That person left it for me to find, and I'm pretty sure they wanted you to see it, too. Whoever this is, they want to tear us apart. They want you to doubt me. And you do—"

He stopped, causing Kate to look down at him. She saw the torment in his eyes, saw the anguish of everything he'd heard and seen since he'd left her at the party.

The party. It seemed so long ago now. So distant and surreal. She remembered the children laughing, remembered her mother's soft encouraging smile. And she remembered all the doubt in her friends' questioning looks, their solemn, sad expressions as they all tried to reassure each other.

Then she remembered that strange clown who'd left her a big plastic daisy. And something tugged at her subconscious, something familiar and close.

With a moan of sheer terror, Kate tugged away from Parker and rushed down the hall toward Brandon's room. She opened the door with such force, it crashed back against the wall, causing Parker to follow her, and causing her son to sit up in bed.

"Mom?"

Unable to speak, Kate could only point toward the dresser where some of Brandon's gifts were scattered. She looked at Parker, then watched as his gaze followed her finger. "That yellow plastic daisy," she said in a shattered whisper. "I found that when I was bringing Brandon's things into his room today."

Parker looked confused and Brandon looked sleepy. His eyes widened when he saw Parker standing in the doorway. "You came!"

But Kate's eyes were still on the gaudy flower. "Parker...uh, Parker just wanted to tell you good night." Motioning to Parker, she pulled him into the room.

Parker leaned over Brandon. "I'm sorry I had to leave the party, Mr. Brandon. An emergency."

"Is everything better now?" Brandon asked through a yawn.

"Everything is better," Parker said, his hand moving over Brandon's hair. "Just wanted to tell you how much fun I had today. And...Happy Birthday."

"Thanks," Brandon said. "It was so awesome and—"

"And you need to go back to sleep," Kate said, her gaze meeting Parker's in the muted light from the hallway. Even though her hands were shaking, she quickly tucked Brandon back in, then she picked up the big flower and hurried into the hallway, Parker right on her heels.

When they were out of earshot of her son, Kate whirled and held the flower up so Parker could see it. "One of the clowns at the party gave a flower like this to me," she said, her voice raw and low. "I put it on a table when I came up to the porch to talk to you. And it wasn't with any of the stuff Brandon and I brought in today. Parker, how did this get from the party to Brandon's bedroom?"

The woman stood outside the gate, smiling to herself. It had been so very easy. Tugging the clown mask off her face, she pushed at her limp, damp hair. Getting inside hadn't been a problem, since several clowns had been hired for the big birthday bash. She'd just kept a close watch on the fun and games supercenter between here and Savannah, rented her own costume, then managed to stow away in one of the hired performers' vans, hidden from sight underneath some blankets and costumes in the back. The unknowing fellow hadn't even bothered to look in the back. Easy.

Of course, being in this ridiculous getup all afternoon

hadn't been so easy. And dealing with screaming, noisy kids wasn't exactly her cup of tea. But she'd managed to leave a few more pieces of evidence inside the mighty Parker Buchanan's private domain. Wouldn't he be surprised when he got home to find something besides leftover balloons and birthday cake waiting for him?

That is, if the police let him come home. Even if Parker didn't find the clues, perky Kate Brooks probably would. She'd even left some pretty little trinkets in Kate's cute cottage, too. And Kate wouldn't even notice that somehow her so-called security guard had missed the whole visit. After all, it was easy to watch and wait until just the right minute to get inside a house.

The way she saw it, Kate would soon put two and two together, because Kate would be so concerned about Parker and his friendly dogs, she was sure to come back here soon enough, but by then Kate would be confused; she would doubt Parker. Kate would begin to believe the man she'd been getting so close to was a cold-blooded killer.

"And I can always tip off the police again."

The local cops were about as brainy as Parker's dogs. But then, they were easy to please, those two big puppies. Just a few treats here and there through the iron fence each time she happened by, and they'd taken a liking to her. Not exactly watchdogs, but then Parker was weak so it figured he'd trained his animals to be docile and kid-friendly.

She headed away from the house, staying in the shadows as she hurried down the road to where she'd left an old used car hidden in the trees last night. And she'd been very careful about being disguised when

she'd gone through the gate, just in case her little
entrance in the van had been recorded. She'd also been
careful last night when she'd called a cab to come and
pick her up at the gas station up the road. So far so good.

"It won't be long now," she reasoned. Her plan was
in its final stages.

THIRTEEN

Monday morning, Kate glanced up from her charts when the security door buzzed. "Yes?" she said into the intercom, her nerves tingling with awareness.

"It's Jennifer. I need to talk to you."

Kate glanced around the enclosed unit. Everything was under control right now. She could take a few minutes. "Let me tell one of the other nurses and I'll be right out."

After making sure the others were aware she was going out into the waiting area, Kate walked through the security doors to where Jennifer paced in front of the elevators.

"I'm so glad I found you," she told Kate, grabbing her by the arm.

Worried by Jennifer's nervous behavior, Kate followed Jennifer around the corner to the waiting area. "What's up?"

Jennifer sat down, then tossed her big purse on a nearby chair. "I heard about Parker becoming a suspect after he talked with the police Saturday."

Kate tried to gauge the look in her friend's eyes. "And—"

"And, in spite of all the rumors, I believe you, Kate. I don't think Parker did this."

Kate let out a hushed breath. "Thank you. That means so much to me." Then she eyed Jennifer again. "I wanted to call everyone after Parker came back from the police station, but I was trying to hold it all together for Brandon's sake. If everyone else doubts Parker, what made you feel this way?"

Jennifer's smile was soft and full of compassion. "Because I was once accused of something I didn't do, so I know how it feels."

Surprised, Kate leaned close. "When?"

Jennifer's brown eyes went even darker. "Oh, never mind. It was a long time ago. I didn't come here to dredge up my past. I wanted to tell you something I heard from one of my parents from the day care. She works at the courthouse and she…well, she hears things. Normally, I wouldn't repeat some of the things she tells me, but after I talked to Dee, I thought we needed to know this. Especially you and Parker."

"What?" Kate asked, her heart pulsing a beat that could probably match the machines helping the tiny babies in the NNICU.

"Something that's been right there in front of us all along," Jennifer said, her voice low. "Penny Brighton. Think about it, Kate. Penny Brighton has the same initials as Parker Buchanan. And according to what this woman told me, the police think that's very interesting. In fact, they're trying to locate Penny so they can question her, too."

She lowered her voice even more. "We know Josie was in that grave, but someone has apparently been posing as her for years now. Remember when Dee got that strange phone call and she had to tell the police about it? Well, that was Shelley, Josie's sister. Dee had to keep quiet about it."

Kate nodded. "But we know all of that now. Shelley thought Josie was alive, but the e-mails and letters she got from Josie didn't make much sense. She got suspicious and called Dee, so Dee reported it and the authorities verified it with Shelley—"

Jennifer interrupted. "Yes, Dee went back over all of that today when I called her with my concerns about Penny. But we still have to keep it quiet. I promised Dee, since leaking this information could jeopardize the case."

Kate looked out the window, watching the billowing clouds floating by in the afternoon sky. "But how can that help Parker? They have the same initials, but so do other people. Penny couldn't have been involved in this, could she? She's been gone for a long time. Besides, she has a beef with the Kesslers, not Parker."

"Are you sure?" Jennifer asked, excitement lighting up her face. "Think about it, Kate. Penny always blamed Parker for the wreck between them that night, even though the police report said it was all her fault. And then she married Steff's brother, Adam Kessler, but after he died, the Kesslers refused to acknowledge her or the baby she claimed was Adam's. What if—"

"What if Penny is the one trying to set up Parker?" Kate said, finishing the statement. She almost told Jennifer about the fake lockets and the sketch Parker had found, but the police had told them to keep that evidence quiet. She knew she could trust Jennifer, but the less her friend knew the better off she'd be right now. "I never thought of that. Penny might be blaming Parker for everything she went through. But why now? From what we know, she refused to have a DNA test done on her child, then she left."

"Exactly," Jennifer replied. "Steff said she left because the Kesslers thought the baby wasn't Adam's. Do you think Parker somehow knew that and now she's afraid of all the attention? Maybe she thinks he'll spill the beans on her if they bring her in for questioning or something?"

"But why would that matter?" Kate asked, searching her mind for Penny's motivation. "It wouldn't matter now if the baby wasn't Adam's. Even if Parker knows that, which I doubt, he can't hurt Penny. She chose to leave." She gasped, her head coming up. "Unless Penny is hiding something else. She was Josie's best friend. She must know something about Josie's death. Something that she doesn't want anyone else to know."

Jennifer nodded. "That's what I'm thinking, too. I wanted to tell you first, before we tell the others. I don't want to get your hopes up, but if we can figure out what's going on with Penny, this could be a break for Parker."

Kate stood up. "You're right. I have to let him know."

"Tell him we need to keep it quiet for now," Jennifer said.

Kate nodded, then decided to be honest with Jennifer. "There's more that I've never told anyone, too. But now it's beginning to make more sense." She explained about giving the police the lockets and the flower she'd found in Brandon's bedroom. "Yesterday, Parker and I turned that over to the police, but we haven't heard anything yet. And he also found a sketch he'd drawn of me years ago—someone had put it inside his car. But they'd also written *PB* in bright red across my face, with a few scratch marks over it for extra emphasis."

"Do the police know that?" Jennifer asked, shock making her face go pale.

Kate thought back over the conversation she and Parker had had with the police the night they'd found the sketch and the flower. They'd immediately called the two detectives to Kate's house. While they'd taken the sketch and the flower in as evidence, Kate didn't pin much hope on the police believing Parker. Nikki had even suggested Parker could have planted the items, just to scare Kate.

"They know everything Parker and I know now." Then she pulled Jennifer close. "Please don't say anything yet. Nikki and Detective Anderson don't seem to believe us, no matter what we say."

"I won't," Jennifer said. "I think we need to keep this quiet until you hear back from the police."

"Yes, the less said the better." Kate hugged Jennifer close. "Thank you, Jennifer, not only for telling me this, but…well, for believing in Parker, too."

Jennifer smiled again. "I have a soft heart, especially when I want one of my friends to be happy. And it seems like if anything good has come out of this grisly murder, at least it's brought all of us back together— some in very romantic ways."

Kate heard her friend's wistful tone. "Well, there's always hope. You might be next."

"I doubt that," Jennifer said with a tight laugh, her brown eyes expressionless. "I don't exactly have time for a relationship these days. And speaking of that, I'm on my lunch break, so I've got to run."

They hugged again, then Jennifer hurried toward the elevator. After leaving Parker a message to call her, Kate went back to work, but her mood had changed considerably.

This might just be the break they needed to clear Parker's name.

The mood of the aged, stooped woman hovering near the entrance to the neonatal unit had taken a turn for the worse. She'd come to leave Kate a nice package, shuffling up and down the hall in the meantime under the guise of being a distant aunt to one of the preemies—if anyone asked. And as luck would have it, she'd been right around the corner when Jennifer had showed up all in a flutter to talk to Kate Brooks. Jennifer Pappas had always been a goody-two-shoes. And now she was messing in things she had no business fooling with. Well, they didn't have any proof of anything. It was all pure speculation. Still, hearing Jennifer's little tidbit of information would serve her well.

Keeping one step ahead of all of these harebrained people was beginning to drain her nerves, but what choice did she have now?

Because Parker Buchanan couldn't get away with this. Not again. She needed him to pay for what he'd done to her. And she was running out of options. Parker was a perfect fall guy. The police might not think he was guilty of murder, but she believed it was possible. She wanted Parker and Kate both to suffer the way she had, and now she wanted Jennifer Pappas to suffer right along with them.

* * *

Kate rushed back to the NNICU, a tempered hope running through her heart as she thought about what this news might do to help Parker's case. Right now, all the police had on him was circumstantial. And until they heard back, Kate just had to hope that he'd be cleared. Kate was determined to make that happen, even if she had to hunt down Penny Brighton herself and get some answers. What if Penny really was the one doing all of this?

Before Kate could put that train of thought into coherent thoughts, one of her coworkers called out. "Hey, Miss Woolgatherer, you've got a present."

Kate glanced to where her coworker was pointing. "What's that?"

"Don't know. But somebody dropped it down at the information desk. It has your name on it. And a note about it being a late birthday present for Brandon."

Kate spun around so fast, a pile of papers on the desk flew out into the air and fell on the floor. Looking up and down the cramped unit, she asked, "Did you happen to see who brought it up?"

"No—just one of the orderlies."

Kate wasn't listening. Instead, she was staring at the brightly wrapped package on her desk, one hand on her roiling stomach. The paper looked familiar. She should know. She'd used it to wrap Brandon's gift for the party. Which meant that whoever had recycled it had been at the party.

"Aren't you gonna open that, girl?"

Kate sank down in her chair, panic holding her still. "Sure. I'm just out of breath. It's been a busy morning."

"Tell me something I don't know. I'm going on my break now that you're back."

Kate nodded, her eyes still on the crudely wrapped package. Did she dare open it? Or should she call the police?

Deciding she couldn't stand not knowing, she carefully pulled at the tape holding the crinkled paper together. Then she gasped as she saw what was inside.

It was one of the Patchman action toys someone had given to Brandon the other day. The toy had been damaged, its face bashed in and cut. Shocked and repulsed, Kate threw the toy down then noticed the white folded parchment inside the package. It was a recent drawing Parker had done of Kate and Brandon— but again, the picture had been slashed over with bright-red ink. And written across the bottom were the words *My little family.*

With the initials PB scrawled underneath.

Either someone was trying very hard to convince Kate that Parker was dangerous, or Penny Brighton had just left another calling card.

"We have to go to the police again," Parker said after Kate arrived at his house in a panic. He held the toy and the sketch in his hands, disgust filling his heart. "The police dusted everything we turned in for prints. But they didn't find anything. They even came here and checked out the entire place, but I don't think they believe me. And I think they'll be back with a warrant to search my personal files. I won't put you and Brandon through that. I have to be upfront with them, for all of our sakes. And they need to know

that you're being targeted at the hospital—that
borders on stalking."

Kate pushed a hand through her hair. She'd come
straight to Parker's house after leaving work. "But what
if they take this the wrong way? What this person is
doing—it implies you want to harm me and now
Brandon, too."

Parker searched her face. She looked exhausted—
and afraid. "Do you think that?"

"Of course I don't," she said. Then she swallowed
and cleared her throat. "Look, I came here right away
to show you this, but also because I found out something
today that makes me believe you *are* being set up."

He pulled her down on an ottoman near the fireplace. "What?"

She told him what Jennifer had repeated to her. "It's
secondhand and could just be part of all the rumors, but
it does make sense. And Shelley Skerritt has cooperated
with the police—that part is fact. She believes someone
has been posing as her sister for years now."

"Penny Brighton." Parker's entire nervous system
went on full alert. "She'd certainly have it in for me."

Kate grabbed his hand. "Because of the accident?"

"Yes. Penny…Penny was always so angry and bitter.
She blamed all the bad in her life on everyone else. At
least that's what Josie used to tell me."

"Did Josie ever say anything about the wreck? About
how it had affected Penny? Or about Penny's baby?"

"I didn't see much of Josie after the wreck. She came
by the hospital once, but it was awkward. She was
friends with the woman who'd basically smashed her
car into mine. I just remember her saying that Penny was

very depressed after the accident. She never once hinted that either of them might be pregnant. Never." He held Kate's hand, marveling at how dainty and delicate she seemed. But she was strong, so strong. He needed that strength now. "Josie seemed so down the last time I saw her. Even though I was the one in the hospital, she didn't look so hot. I guess she had a lot on her mind." And he wished he could have helped her, saved her.

"Penny and Adam Kessler got married because Penny was supposedly pregnant with Adam's baby, but then after Adam died, Penny and Josie both just left," Kate said, trying to remember that summer so long ago. "I heard they went to Europe and Josie stayed there. Then Penny came back with her baby. But she left after the Kesslers wouldn't have anything to do with her." She tapped her fingers on the ottoman. "I guess when she refused to have the DNA test done, she knew she didn't have any other options. But if the baby wasn't Adam's, then who *was* the father?"

Parker stared at the empty fireplace. "Two women, both pregnant just months apart. One of them left with a baby, and the other one is dead and we're not sure about her baby." He shook his head. "Something just doesn't add up."

"None of this makes sense," Kate said.

He looked out the windows at the squirrels frolicking in the backyard. "But…what if…what if Penny *is* behind this? Does that mean she knows something about Josie's death? Or possibly, Josie's missing baby?"

Kate let out a breath. "Maybe she does, and maybe she truly believes you might have had something to do with it. I mean, if she and Josie were best friends—well,

Josie might have confided in her, given her a reason to target you. She's obviously been monitoring all the chatter on the alumni loop and Web site. She would have to hear all the speculation and rumors." She let out a visible shudder. "And she has to be the one leaving all these creepy packages for us. But why wouldn't she just come forward and talk to the police?"

Parker couldn't answer that. It only brought up more questions. "But what would she know about me? I know Josie's baby wasn't mine. And where *is* the baby? The police didn't find a second skeleton." He bent his head. "I can't even think about it—a tiny baby buried somewhere. If I thought in my heart that child belonged to me and was still alive, I'd be out searching for it. I wouldn't stop, Kate. You know that, don't you?"

Kate touched a hand to his face. "I do. I do." Then she pulled him close. "We have to get through this. We have to find the truth."

He held her there, savoring the warmth of her arms around him. He hadn't needed companionship before, hadn't thought much about the loneliness deep inside his soul. But now, he couldn't imagine his life without Kate and Brandon.

"I can't lose you," he said, his whisper touching on her soft, warm skin. "I won't lose you."

"No," Kate said, smiling through her tears. "Not many people get a second chance. But we have. I won't lose you, either."

"Then we take this to the police?"

She nodded. "Just let me call Jennifer and make sure she can take Brandon home with her when the day care closes. I don't want him to hear about this."

"I agree." He tugged her up off the ottoman.

Kate brushed at her scrubs. "Maybe I should go home and change first."

Parker smiled over at her, then reached up to push a finger through her hair. "You look cute to me. Who knew teddy bears and lollipops could be so interesting."

"It's for the babies," she replied. "Those tiny little premature babies." Then she caught his hand in hers. "Parker—"

"I know what you're thinking. There might be a child out there somewhere. A child that doesn't know his real mother is dead." He ran a hand through his hair. "And that he or she has a father somewhere."

"Parker," she said again, her voice catching.

"We'll find the child, Kate. Somehow, we have to find out if that child is still alive. If Penny is behind this, maybe she'll at least tell the police the truth about that."

Kate prayed he was right. For the child's sake, at least. And for Parker's sake.

If Penny Brighton knew something, she needed to step forward. Kate wouldn't rest until she could make that happen.

FOURTEEN

Two days later, Parker walked up to the stately Victorian house on the tree-lined street near the college campus. Telling himself he could do this, he leaned on his cane then knocked on the double doors of Thatcher and Grace Duncan's house.

"You promised Brandon," he reminded himself, a steely resolve that he usually saved for his comic-book character's motivation making him hold tightly to his cane.

Kate was in some kind of emergency with premature twins. Her frantic call had been loud and clear. She needed him. That thought alone was the only thing keeping him on solid ground these days. Kate needed him.

"Parker, I'm so glad I caught you. I can't get away for a few hours. But I need you to do me a favor since I can't get home."

Even though he had a guard posted on Kate around the clock, he still felt his heart drop to his feet. "Of course. What is it?"

"Please go to my mother's house and get Brandon. Jennifer dropped him off there from day care because he's supposed to go on a church field trip tonight, but I won't be able to take him. Bowling, I think. My mother has some sort of meeting she can't miss, yet she insists she needs to be the one to take Brandon on this outing. I've tried to tell her that's not necessary, but she's laying a big guilt trip on me. But she hates bowling and Thatch is out of town. Parker, please. I need to know Brandon will be safe on this trip. If you're with him, I can rest easy."

"Okay, just slow down. Are you all right?"

He heard her shifting sigh. "I will be when I see you and Brandon, but that will have to wait. One of our mothers just went through an emergency C-section. Twins, and they aren't doing so great. The night nurse called in sick so I have to wait until we can call someone to take over the shift. I can't leave right now, but I promised Brandon I'd help chaperone. I know things are tough for us, and you probably don't want to deal with a lot of public scrutiny, but please, Parker?"

How could he say no to that?

"Kate, I'll do it. Just give me your mother's address."

She rattled off the house number and street. "Oh—my mother is going to try and talk you out of this. She's gone all self-righteous on me about things. Don't give in. I trust you with Brandon. I know you'll take care of him."

Kate needed him and she trusted him, in spite of everything that had happened over the last few days. They had only been frustrated by the stalled-out police investigation. Even after he and Kate had gone to the police with all their suspicions, not one shred of evidence could be pinned on Penny Brighton. The woman seemed to have disappeared off the face of the earth. No one could locate her or her parents, if her parents were still alive. She'd covered her tracks, that was for sure. And none of the things they'd found at his home or Kate's had produced any viable prints. The police had suggested that they could trace where the red ink used on the sketches had probably come from—Parker's own collection of drawing pens. Which meant the police were still skeptical and still suspicious of Parker, since there was no way to prove Penny was the one doing all the dirty work.

So now, here he stood, wondering if he could live up to Kate's expectations. But he'd called here earlier and talked to Brandon and he'd promised the boy he'd be here to take him to the bowling alley. It was a tough promise to honor, considering everyone there would probably be shocked to find the latest "person of interest" in a murder case showing up at a youth outing. It didn't matter that the police had confirmed they'd only questioned Parker and that he wasn't being accused of anything. He certainly knew how the world worked. People judged too quickly and too harshly, without having the facts.

Parker glanced around to make sure no one was lurking about outside the house. He hated being on guard all the time, but he didn't want to put Brandon in harm's way. He didn't see anything out of the ordinary on the picturesque street lined with live oaks and magnolias.

A plump maid with fluffy white hair opened the door, her smile indulgent, her expression curious. "Mr. Buchanan?"

"Yes. I'm here to get Brandon."

Then he heard fast footsteps pounding against the gleaming hardwood floor of the central hallway. "Mr. Parker, you came!"

Brandon lunged into Parker, almost knocking him off balance.

"Whoa there, Mr. Brandon. Slow down. We've got plenty of time."

The click-click of a woman's heels followed. "Daphne, please show Mr. Buchanan in. I'd like to have a word with him before Brandon leaves."

Parker heard the firm tone in that pleasant request. No doubt he was about to get a good talking-to from a concerned mother and grandmother. And how could he blame Grace? His picture and name had been plastered all over the local news and in the daily paper. He'd even seen Dee Owens and Stephanie Kessler on the evening news, fielding questions about him at a press conference that had been set up to defend the college. Thankfully, both had reinforced that he wasn't being held and he hadn't been charged with anything. He was just being questioned. They were all being questioned, Dee reminded the reporters.

But even that show of solidarity couldn't stop him from being publicly judged and condemned. Even though Kate's mother had gushed over him at the party, after hearing the details of his friendship with Josie Skerritt and about the initials on the locket, Grace Duncan had probably amended how she felt about him.

The maid guided him into the sparkling clean, antique-filled house. Grace stood at the bottom of the winding staircase, near an elaborate marble-topped hall table that displayed a crystal bowl full of floating camellia blossoms. "Hello, Mr. Buchanan."

Parker took in the carefully styled hair and the cashmere sweater with pearls. "Mrs. Duncan, how are you?"

"I'm fine, all things considered." She smiled down

at Brandon. "Go on, honey, and get your jacket. Daphne will help you find it."

She waited until Brandon and the maid were gone, then motioned toward a formal parlor on the left. "Let's sit in here for a minute."

Parker followed, the thud of his cane, this one topped off with a pewter wood duck, finding cadence with the click of Grace's pumps. "Thank you, Mrs. Duncan."

"Call me Grace."

It was a regal command.

"Grace," he said as he managed to sit down on a high-backed Queen Anne sofa, his bad leg stiff but tingling with nervous energy.

Grace took her time straightening her pleated wool skirt, then smiled over at him, her blue eyes shimmering like ice chips. "I'll be honest. Considering the new developments in this college murder case, I do not approve of Kate asking you to go on this outing with Brandon. But she seems to have unyielding trust in you, and she is the child's mother. So you will take care of my only grandson, won't you, Mr. Buchanan?"

"Call me Parker."

It was a firm request.

"Parker, I expect you to do right by Brandon and Kate."

"I understand. I'll watch out for Brandon tonight. You have my word on that."

"Oh, I'm sure you will. But I don't just mean tonight."

Parker saw the mother's determination in her eyes. "Look…Grace. I care about your daughter. A lot. And Brandon—well, what's not to love about that little boy?"

"We all love him," she replied, a new respect sparking in her eyes. But beyond that respect, he could also see a valid concern. "You understand—people are talking—"

"I didn't have anything to do with this murder," Parker interrupted, meeting her gaze straight on. "That's the truth, Grace. No matter what people are saying, no matter what you've heard or seen on the news, I'm innocent." He held his hands out, palms up. "I can't prove that, but at least Kate believes me. However, if you feel uncomfortable with me being around your grandson, then I guess we can both explain to Brandon why I can't go bowling with him tonight. And I'll leave."

When he didn't flinch or look away, Grace finally nodded. "I believe you." Then she stood in dismissal. "However, you need to remember that my husband is a retired district court judge with many, many contacts within law enforcement and the entire court system of Georgia, and if I ever find out you've not been completely honest with me or my daughter, no court in this country will save you. Are we clear on that?"

Parker marveled at her serene smile. "Yes, ma'am. Very clear." Then he stood to look down at her, his smile tight and sure in spite of the tremor of his heart. "I'm going to tell you something that I've never told anyone, not even Kate." At the lift of her brows, he hurried on. "The night I had the accident that left me crippled, I was on my way to find Kate and tell her that I wanted to date her."

Grace clasped a hand to her pearls. "Really?"

"Yes, and now I'm going to tell you the rest of that story. That first date never happened, but now Kate and I have another chance. This time around, we've really gotten to know each other. And I love your daughter. I've always loved her, but now that love is strong and sure, because Kate and Brandon have shown me what real love is all about. They've shown me God's love."

Grace actually sank back down on her chair, her fingers clutching the peach-and-sage brocade cushions. "Oh, my."

"I would do anything to protect them. Anything," Parker said, his tone low and serious. And just to reassure her, he added, "I've hired a security guard to stay near Kate, both at work and at home. She doesn't want people to know that, but I wanted you to know, because I need you to believe me."

"I believe you," Grace said, her expression softening. "I truly do."

"Good," Parker replied, relief washing over him. Then he leaned close. "But I'd like to be the one to tell Kate that I love her. Don't spoil it for me."

Grace actually fluttered her lashes like a schoolgirl. "Far be it from me to get in the way of true love."

"I'm glad we've reached this understanding," Parker said, offering her his hand.

She took it as she stood. "Have a good time with my grandson, Parker. Watch after him." Then she squeezed his hand. "And hold your head up. If you have nothing to hide, you have to act that way."

Brandon came rushing back into the room then. "Let's go. Mr. Parker, can you help me bowl?"

"I'll do my best," Parker replied, grinning down at Brandon.

"Bye, Grandma."

"Goodbye, darling," Grace said, her eyes still on Parker. "Brandon, take care of your friend here, okay?"

"Okay," Brandon said through a giggle.

Parker nodded to Grace, then headed off behind Brandon.

At least he now had one formidable ally on his side. And he had a feeling before this was all over, he was going to need her.

They made it to the bowling alley on the other side of town just in time to meet the group at the doors. Once the chaperones and kids were herded inside, the minister held up a hand to silence all the giggling, excited children, then looked over the crowd, nodding to each of the grown-ups.

Parker tried to ignore the pointed stares of some of the others. For Brandon's sake, he took Grace's advice and did hold his head high. He knew the truth about himself. And he prayed the truth about this murder would come out very soon so he could get on with the life he planned with Kate and Brandon.

As if sensing his need to find solace in God's grace, Reverend Rogers looked right at Parker. "Parker, would you lead us in prayer, please?"

Parker was as shocked as some of the other adults. He heard gasps of surprise rippling through the group with the same crashing as the balls and pins hitting together down in the pits. His first inclination was to decline. He'd never prayed publicly in his life. He'd rarely even prayed privately. But lately, with Kate's gentle example, he'd been learning to pray again.

So he took a breath, nodded, then smiled down at Brandon. The little boy reached out his hand to Parker. Touched, Parker took the small trusting hand in his, then glanced around at the now-silent group. "I'd be glad to do that, Reverend."

Everyone bowed their heads and Parker did the same, closing his eyes to give him courage. Holding onto Brandon, he began. "Dear God, thank You for bringing us together here tonight to have some fun. Thank You for these children and their parents and all those who love them. Help us to keep them safe, help us to understand that life isn't always easy. Help us, Lord, through the storms, the troubles and tragedies of life." He paused, overcome with a longing so great that it seemed to pierce his soul. "Help *me,* Lord, to understand that each fight is one more step toward Your love and understanding. I ask for Your power and Your strength to guide me through all things. Amen."

When he opened his eyes, Reverend Rogers was looking at him, a soft smile of understanding on his face. "Thank you, Parker. And welcome."

Parker had just accepted Christ into his heart, in a bowling alley, with a little boy holding his hand. And even with the doubters here amongst them, he'd managed to declare his faith and ask for God's help. A sense of peace settled over him. He understood that no matter what the future might bring, he had someone on his side. He'd get through this; he'd survive somehow.

"Wow," he said as he watched Brandon run over to the service desk to get his bowling shoes.

"Wow is right," the minister said, clasping a hand on Parker's back. "I've heard all about everything in your life, from too many concerned citizens even to count. But Kate vouches for you, so that's good enough for me. I've prayed for you and Kate, and I do believe the Lord has heard my prayers. It took a lot of courage to come here, and especially to do what you just did. I'm proud of you, son."

Parker looked down at the worn red carpet at his feet. "I've certainly never done that before. I mean— I've been hidden away for so long—"

"Feels good to come out of hiding, doesn't it?"

"It sure does." Then he looked over, searching for the compassion in the minister's eyes. "Do you believe me, sir?"

The minister shook his head, causing Parker's heart to tremble. "No, son, I believe *in* you. There is a difference, you know."

Parker grinned then. "I think I do. Kate said that very same thing to me recently." He reached out to shake the minister's hand. "And I appreciate you standing up for me."

"Part of my job. I love bringing lost sheep back into the flock. And from what our lovely Kate had told me, you've been lost for some time now."

Parker couldn't deny that. "I guess I have. But you know what's strange about all of this? I've finally found a woman I can spend the rest of my life with, but my future is not so secure right now. How do I deal with that?"

"You keep right on praying, son," the minister said. "You pray through all of it. The truth will come out. It won't be easy or fast, but the truth will come out."

"Kate says God always has a plan for us, we just can't see it sometimes."

"Kate is not only pretty, but she's smart, too. If you put God in your plans, He will always show you the way."

Parker lifted his head in acknowledgment. "I'd better go and help Brandon get started."

"Have fun," Reverend Rogers said. "Now let me see if I can continue my tradition of bowling a perfect game."

Parker shifted around on his cane. "Really?"

"Nah, not really. But even a preacher can dream, right?"

"Right." Parker laughed at the sparkle in the preacher's eyes.

Then he hurried toward where Brandon was waiting with his team of tiny bowlers. "Ready to get this going?" Parker asked, grinning down at Brandon.

"Yep. I just wish Mom was here."

"Me, too," Parker said, hoping he'd get to talk to her when he took Brandon home later. In spite of the uncertainty of his future right now, his heart seemed to be overflowing with hope. He had so much he wanted to say to her.

FIFTEEN

Kate pulled into the driveway of her house, her heart radiating with a sense of both joy and dread when she saw the porch light on and Parker's car parked by the carport, the ever-present security car hovering on the street.

Parker had brought Brandon home and stayed with him, and while she was so glad that Parker was here waiting for her, she hated the dark clouds hanging over them. But she had to keep the faith; she had to believe that God would see them through. And somehow, she had to help Parker clear his name.

She was beginning to love Parker Buchanan.

Beginning? She laid her head on the steering wheel, wondering exactly when she had fallen in love with Parker. Maybe way back in college, if she tried to be honest about things. But back then, she'd had the single-minded, impulsive dream of being a Nashville star. That dream had changed her life and given her Brandon, so she couldn't regret it. But it had also cost her ten years away from Parker.

Reminding herself that she'd told Parker they'd needed those years apart, that it might have been part of God's plan in their lives, Kate let out a sigh and tried to accept that this was how it was supposed to have been. Now, she was much more sensible than she'd been right out of college, and her faith in God was so much stronger. Now, she could appreciate Parker for the man he'd become, not just the friend she remembered.

"It's not too late for us, Parker," she said as she got out of the car, every bone in her body rattling with a soul-weary heaviness as she glanced around the quiet street, then nodded toward the guard in the car. Or at least, it wouldn't be too late if they could find out the truth. Pushing the edgy, reckless thoughts out of her mind, she was determined to be upbeat for Parker's sake.

He opened the door the minute she stepped on the porch. Then he opened his arms.

Kate hurried to him, glad for the warmth of his embrace. "Hi," she said against the spicy smell of his sweater.

"Hi, yourself." He stood back, his hands on her shoulders, his eyes full of understanding. "I'll make you some tea."

Touched that he sensed exactly what she needed right now, Kate followed him into the kitchen, noting that he'd limped to the door and back without his cane. "How's Brandon?"

"He's sleeping away." Parker turned after setting the kettle on the burner. "We got him in his pajamas and he brushed his teeth, then we went over his spelling words." He stopped, his hand on the sugar bowl. "And we said our prayers."

Tears pricked at Kate's eyes. "Thank you."

She watched, content and secure, as Parker made her an elaborate grilled cheese sandwich, then thin-sliced an apple to go with it. But she wasn't sure she could eat a bite of it. "You didn't have to do that."

"You need to eat." He tilted his head toward the big pot on the stove. "I raided the fridge and cabinets and made vegetable soup, too."

Now Kate knew she was truly in love. A man who cooked without even having to be asked. "You are too kind."

He turned from his duties to grasp her hand in his. "I'm not that kind, I just needed to keep busy. And I want to take care of you."

She saw the unspoken promise there in his eyes. Did he love her in the same way she loved him? Wanting to spill her heart, she refrained. They still had other things to push through. They needed to go over the details of this mess until something made sense.

She waited until he'd dished up soup for both of them before she tackled the subject they'd been avoiding. "Parker, we need to talk."

He gave her an appraising look. "So you said earlier. And I have something to tell you, too. First, how are the twins?"

"I think they'll pull through. It'll take months, though. They only weighed about a pound and a half each." She closed her eyes, then said a quick blessing for the food, thanking God for helping her to minister to the precious infants she'd monitored over the last few hours. And she thanked Him for Parker, then asked Him to help them, help them all.

"Eat a bit, then we'll talk," Parker said when she lifted her head, his spoon pointed toward her steaming soup.

Kate nibbled at the sandwich, then took a couple of

spoonfuls of the hearty soup. "You should open your own restaurant."

"I only want to feed you and Brandon."

As good as the food was, her next bite lodged in her throat. "Parker, what are we going to do next? My mother is worried about us. Did she give you any grief?"

His smile was lopsided and wry. "If you mean did she try to bully me away from you, the answer is yes, sort of. I'm not so easy to bully, however. We had a good talk, and I believe we reached a truce. But I'd never want to get on her bad side, that's for sure." His fingers drumming softly against the counter, he said, "Oh, and by the way, I said the prayer tonight at the bowling alley."

Kate dropped her soupspoon. "You did?"

He looked down at the counter. "Uh-huh. And Kate, for the first time, I got it. I mean, really got it, about what it means to truly give your heart to God."

Kate felt a lump forming in her throat. "Oh, Parker. I'm so glad."

He glanced around, then his eyes settled on her. "Do you think I'm doing this just because I'm in so much trouble?"

She took his hand. "You were in trouble after the accident, but you didn't turn to God then."

"No, because I blamed Him. But now, I need Him." He pulled away, then held up a hand. "But it's not so much to help me out of this trouble. It's more because, well, I've seen your faith and how it gives you this amazing strength. I want that, too. I need that, no matter what kind of trouble I get into. I need the Lord in my life."

Grabbing his hand back, Kate laughed, tears forming in her eyes. "This is so amazing."

"Yeah, and you should have seen the looks I got at the bowling alley. But it's okay. I can handle it now."

Kate breathed a sigh of relief at that. "I'm glad, because this will probably get worse before it gets better. But we can't give up. Jennifer called me again today."

"Did *she* try to bully *you* into ditching me?"

"No, exactly the opposite. She agrees with us that you might be getting set up to take the fall for Josie's murder. And she still thinks Penny is behind it, too. Now if we could just prove that." She nibbled a bite of apple. "I'm so sure Penny is lurking about, it gives me the creeps. I intend to watch for her from now on, though. If she shows up again at the hospital, I hope I can catch her red-handed."

Parker came around to sit down beside her. Although he was more than willing to confront Penny, he didn't want Kate doing that. "No, Kate. Don't go getting too brave for your own good. We have to let the police do their jobs."

Kate couldn't wait for the police. "Right, while Penny Brighton could possibly be getting away with murder? And framing you for it?"

He didn't argue with her. "Okay, I know you want to go back over everything, so let's start with Penny and me. It makes sense that she could be the one harassing us. Penny always blamed me for the accident. And since you've been trying to track people on the Web site, and since you and I have been seen around town together, she'd have to have noticed. She must have been at Brandon's party, so that means she's smart and cunning. Maybe someone else tipped her off about you taking over the site, but she could easily be posting under a different name, so she would know all the activity going on there."

Kate bobbed her head. "I have gotten a couple of cryptic questions on there."

"We need to go over all the archives and see what we can find—a pattern or a certain screen name, then we can remind the police, too." He took a sip of water. "Before we knew for sure that the skeleton was Josie, we couldn't locate Penny or Josie. But now that we know Josie is dead, who's been posing as Josie on the e-mail all this time? It could be Penny. And Jennifer heard from the woman at the courthouse that the police are interested in talking to Penny. Maybe Penny's heard this, too, and she's starting to panic?"

Kate pushed away her food. "Especially if she's been hanging around, stalking us. Parker, she's obviously been in your house and mine." Folding her arms across her chest, Kate shuddered again. "It just gives me the creeps. I mean, whoever's been doing this is just plain crazy and delusional."

Parker grabbed one of her hands, his fingers playing over her knuckles. "Penny was a loose cannon even back in college. And think about it—she's been widowed, shunned and exiled since then. We can't know what she's been through all this time. That could cause a person to go off the deep end."

"She's desperate," Kate said, the warmth of his hand soothing her crackling nerves.

"And dangerous." Kate saw the warning shining in his eyes. "Which is why I think you and Brandon should either come to my house, or at least go and stay with your mother and the judge."

Kate saw the worry in his eyes. "I can't do that. I won't disrupt Brandon's life that way. And we already have a rotating shift of guards outside."

"Then I'll put surveillance cameras around your house."

"Parker, I can't let you do that—"

"Do it for Brandon," he interrupted. "If Penny truly is here in Magnolia Falls, she might start targeting him, too. Someone's already been in your house, Kate. If it was Penny, she deliberately left that flower in Brandon's room. We can't predict what she might do next."

"No, you're scaring me," she said, getting up so quickly the dishes rattled.

Parker was right there, turning her to face him, anger clouding his eyes. "Good. I want to scare you. Because I'm scared *for* you. I'll do whatever we need to do—hire extra guards if I need to. We can't count on the police, Kate. Even if they suspect Penny, too, they don't believe us. They don't believe me. I can't rest knowing you're in danger." He kissed her on the top of her head. "We've got a guard to watch your house, but we need to do more. What if I pick Brandon up from school and day care, so you won't worry about him?"

Too tired to deal with any of it, Kate slumped against him. "I don't know what to do anymore. I don't—"

He lifted her chin, his hand holding her face. "Let me help you. Let me take care of you."

His kiss persuaded her more than mere words ever could. She wanted to feel safe; she wanted to sleep the peaceful sleep of someone who didn't have a care in the world. She wanted this to be over. She pulled away, nodding. "Okay, all right. But—"

Parker interrupted her protests again. "I would take you both home with me, but I don't want people to talk."

"They already are," she reminded him.

"Well, let them talk. We haven't done anything wrong. I'm just trying to protect you."

Kate loved him for his honor and his kindness.

She had to save him from all of this. Somehow.

"Maybe we should just leave town," he said. "You could take a few days off work."

"I…I probably need to but I can't do that either—I wouldn't want anything to happen at the hospital—" She stopped, shaking her head. "I can't believe Penny has been there. We get people in and out all the time, but we're very careful. The security is tight, and yet she still managed to get that package to me." Kate felt sick, so sick and weak she had to sit down. "And she's probably been there before. But how many times?"

Parker didn't waste time answering that. "I'll be right back," he said as he hurried toward the front door.

Kate got up to follow him, then watched as he went out to the car on the road. In a matter of minutes, a stocky woman dressed in a dark uniform followed Parker inside the house. "Hi, I'm Wanda Dotson."

Parker thanked the woman and explained the situation to Kate. "I offered Wanda double her salary to stay inside the house with you overnight." Then he turned back to Wanda. "We have reason to believe Ms. Brooks is being stalked. Just keep an eye on her while you're here, and I'll talk to the day-shift guard about this, too, in case she's home during the day."

Kate looked from Parker to the stoic guard. "I don't think that's necessary—"

"I'll be glad to sleep right here on the couch," the no-nonsense woman said. "I don't put up with a child being in danger."

Kate thanked Wanda, then sent Parker a grateful smile. "Okay, all right. I would feel better knowing someone is here to help me keep my son safe." After Wanda went to the kitchen to "get the lay of the land," Kate turned back to Parker. "Thank you. I don't know how to repay you."

He held a finger to her lips. "You can repay me by being very careful." Then he pulled her close. "I don't want to leave you," he said, his hand on her face.

"I'll be fine. I feel safe." Then she leaned close. "I certainly wouldn't want to mess with Wanda."

"She's a strong woman, that's for sure." He grinned then whispered in her ear. "I asked for a female, because I didn't want any other man around you all the time. But I never dreamed they'd send an Amazon."

Kate slapped his arm. "Thank you."

He kissed her good-night. "I'll call you tomorrow."

"And what about you?" Kate asked, worried about him going back to that big house. "Will you be safe?"

"I have the system in place and since the party, I've added reinforcements. It's like Fort Knox out there."

"I hope so." She waved goodbye, then turned to go and find her new keeper.

In the meantime, Kate prayed, her eyes tightly shut to the dark night. And to the dangers she could sense out there.

"I don't like this, Kate."

Kate held the phone tightly to her ear to keep her

hands from shaking. It had been a couple of days since Wanda had become a fixture around her house, so she'd decided to call Grace to warn her. "Mother, I'm fine. Brandon is safe. We have a security guard right here with us every night."

"But if there is a crazy person out there stalking you, why wouldn't you want to come and stay with Thatch and me?"

Kate couldn't explain her reasoning, except to say that she needed to stick to her routine. "Parker is being framed for this murder," she said. "If anyone notices I've changed my routine, things could get even worse for both of us. So I think it's best that I just go about my business. I'll be careful, I promise. But I'm hoping the culprit won't be as careful and we can end this thing soon."

"Well, whoever it is will notice a strange woman staying at your house."

"Yes, but that should keep whoever it is *out* of my house, I hope. And we have tight security at the hospital. I'm escorted to my car every day anyway. Now, I'll just request a guard going into work, too. And Parker is going to pick Brandon up from school on the days I can't."

"Darling, I understand your commendable sense of loyalty to this man, but what if you're wrong? What if he's not being honest with you?"

"I thought you were past that."

"Well, I must admit he seems sincere. I can see the man is head over heels for you, but I'm just so worried. We hear things, and Thatch says the police still don't have any solid leads. They won't even give him any information."

"They're supposedly looking for Penny Brighton," Kate said, going over once again her theory regarding

Penny. "That makes the most sense, Mother. And until they find her, we're all in danger. So keep this quiet for your own sake. Everyone who's helped out with that Web site has had odd things happen to them, so someone who knows all of us and follows our routines and activities is watching us. And Jennifer and I think it's Penny."

"That girl always was wild and out of control. Remember, even in high school she acted out," Grace said. "Her poor mother used to ask for prayers for her just about every single Sunday."

"She needs our prayers," Kate replied. "But if she tries anything with Parker or Brandon, she'll need more than that."

"Now don't go off on some sort of noble mission, honey," Grace warned. "You just sit tight there and stay close to Parker. And my grandson."

In spite of the serious situation, Kate had to smile. "Oh, so now you want me to stick with Parker after all?"

"Well, when you use that kind of logic, yes, I guess I do," Grace retorted. "Just keep in touch, okay?"

"I promise, I'll call you every day," Kate said. "The police know the situation and while they don't entirely believe us, Penny has moved up on their suspect list."

"And what about my grandson? Is he safe at school?"

"We've talked to the principal and since the school has security anyway, they're aware of the problem," Kate said. "I didn't want to scare Brandon, so I just explained that we were having a visitor for a few days. Wanda decided not to wear her uniform, so he wouldn't get confused or scared. And she likes to cook and clean, so he actually thinks she's a housekeeper. And I hope this stalker will think the same and stay away because of the risk of being exposed."

"I'm getting chills," Grace said. "I won't sleep a wink until this is over."

"Mother, try not to worry. And remember to keep this quiet. We have enough rumors and half-truths out there regarding this case as it is."

Were they on to her?

She'd seen the car pulled up by Kate's house late the other night. She wasn't stupid. Someone was staying at Kate's house. A woman. But why?

Did they have any clue who was leaving them the sketches and other little trinkets? Did they know the plan?

The sketches were Parker's. He could be the one playing little tricks on Kate, couldn't he?

She hoped the police thought that at least. But she'd have to hurry up and get this over with before they figured things out.

The woman sat on the bench just off the college campus, remembering all the bad things she'd ever had to endure in this sleepy little college town. Magnolia Falls College looked so pristine and proper on the outside. But she knew the truth. She knew how people lied and hid their real faces from the world. She knew the rot and decay hidden deep inside those ancient walls. She knew where the body had been buried, too.

They would all pay for messing up her life, for lying and cheating and covering up the truth.

But aren't you doing that very thing now?

Letting out a grunt of disgust, she wondered where

she'd gone wrong. Up until the discovery of that body, things had been rolling right along.

Well, that wasn't exactly the truth. She'd been miserable and lonely for years now. She hated her life. She hated how everything she'd tried to do had failed.

But it all came back to Parker. It had all begun that night, that horrible night when she'd been rejected and ridiculed by the one person she'd thought she could count on. In her mind, she'd lost everything. And she'd had to take drastic measures to try and win her life back—the life she should have had.

Someone had to pay for what had happened that night.

Might as well be Parker. He was a loner, a recluse. Who would miss him? He'd been in self-imposed exile for years now, so what would it matter if he took the fall for this mess? No one would miss Parker Buchanan.

But Parker Buchanan sure would miss Kate Brooks.

He'd miss her and he'd suffer, sitting in a prison cell. He'd suffer the way she'd had to suffer all these years. Then she would be even with Parker. And even if she could never get back the life she'd dreamed about, at least she'd have some sort of satisfaction, knowing everyone blamed him for not one but two murders.

But first, she had to figure out how to kill Kate Brooks.

SIXTEEN

Parker sat in the back of the church, listening to Kate's solo. Her beautiful voice filled the quiet sanctuary, lifting up to the rafters with a sweet release. Her song of joy and redemption seemed to fill Parker's soul with a love so strong and fierce, he wondered how to handle it.

But he was here, inside this old church, watching the woman he loved practicing for the upcoming Easter service. Funny how a man could change, little by little, in small degrees, with each touch, each kiss, each whisper of a prayer. Funny how faith was beginning to be such an important part of his life.

Because of Kate and Brandon.

He felt a light tap on his arm, then turned to find his two friends from the police department sitting behind him.

"How's it going, Parker?" Nikki Rivers asked, her smile as serene as always even though her eyes stayed purposely blank.

"I was fine until you two showed up," Parker said in a low whisper. He glanced up to see if Kate had spotted them, but she had finished her song and was now laughing and talking with the rest of the choir. "What's wrong now?"

Jim Anderson leaned back, then gazed up toward the altar. "We just wanted to talk to you. You know, since you and Kate seem bent on this stalker angle."

"And you two still don't believe us, right?"

Jim glanced at his partner, then back to Parker. "Let's just say, your theory is beginning to make more sense now."

"Because?"

Nikki leaned close. "Because we've tracked down Penny's parents. They're in an old folks' home near Charleston. Seems they haven't seen or heard from their only daughter for a while now. At least not since last summer."

Parker twisted around. "That's when the skeleton was first discovered."

"Bingo," Nikki said. "She went missing soon after. Last known address was in Charleston, but she left her house there locked up tight. Didn't leave a forwarding address." Then she shrugged. "That's all we could get out of them. They seem bent on protecting her and their granddaughter."

That caught Parker's attention. "Did you find Penny's child?"

"Not exactly," Jim said. "We're still looking. Grandparents have her in an exclusive boarding school somewhere near Charleston, but they refuse to give us any information on the kid."

Glancing up at the choir, Parker looked for Kate, but she had her back turned, talking to the choir director. "We need to tell Kate this."

"We'll fill her in," Nikki said. "We just wanted you to know that we're trying to locate Penny Brighton, but that doesn't mean you're off the hook."

"We have every reason to believe Penny is deliberately baiting *us*," Parker said, thinking he'd keep repeating that until they believed him. "She's trying to blame me for this."

Nikki crossed her arms. "We've tested everything you turned in—the sketches, the plastic flower and the lockets, but we just can't seem to connect any of those items to Penny Brighton. Your prints are stamped all over the sketches, of course. And we've matched the drawing pen back to you, too. The red ink is a perfect match to one of your own pen sets."

"Of course," Parker replied, thinking he'd told them as much the first time they'd questioned him. "And the flower?"

"Can't be positive there. We're still waiting for a complete analysis from the state lab."

Jim inclined his head. "If—and this is a big if—if Penny Brighton did plant those items, she didn't leave any traces. Not even on the toy lockets."

"And what about the real locket?" Parker asked. "Did you find anything on the one that was apparently buried with Josie's body?"

"Nope, not much to go on there either. We're sending that one back to the lab for a closer look now, however."

"Then why did you come to church to harass me?"

Nikki shrugged. "We tried calling you. Then we just cruised around until we saw your car. Never dreamed we'd see you here of all places. Interesting, how you're turning over a new leaf right in the middle of all this."

Parker stood up, not bothering to explain to them he'd just been thinking along those same lines. Of course, for very different reasons. "Yeah, isn't it?" Then he leaned over the pew. "Interesting, too, how you still want to pin this on me, when we all know Penny is behind this. But hey, that doesn't surprise me. I guess I'll just have to keep watching and waiting until she makes her next move. Then I'll haul her in myself."

Jim Anderson stood, too. "Don't go doing anything stupid."

"Then why don't you do your jobs?" Parker asked, his question heated with frustration and aggravation. "I can understand that things look bad for me, but Kate deserves the truth, even if you don't believe me."

"Good point," Nikki countered. "That's why we're keeping an eye on you. For Kate's sake."

"Thanks," Parker replied, determined to prove them both wrong. "I'll keep that in mind while I worry about Kate and her son."

Jim halted him with a hand. "Parker, we have to look at the facts. We came here to tell you we're beginning to see things your way. But until we can prove that, we have to keep you on our list. Just hang in there. And keep your cool."

Parker watched them leave, then turned around to look for Kate. He saw several other choir members lingering near the side entrance.

But Kate was nowhere to be found.

Anxious to find part of her sheet music, Kate left ahead of the other choir members to hurry back to the choir room. She'd forgotten part of it when they'd come into the sanctuary to practice and she needed to go over the solo the director had asked her to practice in preparation for next week's rehearsal.

Flipping on the light, she saw her music by her regular chair. If she hurried, she could be back inside the sanctuary before Parker ever missed her. They'd given Wanda a night off so they could have a quiet dinner together. At least Brandon was safe and secure having dinner with her mother and the judge at Terra Cottage. Brandon loved lasagna almost as much as he loved pizza, even if Grace insisted on taking him to eat it at a fancy Italian restaurant instead of the more casual Burt's.

While Kate was looking forward to dinner alone with Parker so she could tell him about some of the latest information she and Jennifer had found, she also wanted to get home and check the alumni Web site. She didn't want to worry Parker and she hadn't been able to talk earlier since Brandon had been with them, but she'd posted a challenge there. A challenge she hoped Penny would see and act upon. Kate was tired of feeling like a victim. So, using herself as bait, she'd attempted to lure Penny out into the open.

I know someone out there is trying to send us a message. If anyone has information that can help solve Josie Skerritt's murder, please contact me privately. I'm ready to listen. And if anyone knows why Parker would have any reason to hurt Josie, talk to me. I want to help. We need to find the real murderer. It's time to stop clowning around.

She'd thrown down the gauntlet. Now she prayed Penny would read that last line and answer the challenge, since Kate felt very strongly that Penny had indeed been at Brandon's party, dressed as a clown. Kate needed answers. And she needed them now. If Penny was as smart as she seemed to be, she'd understand what Kate was asking. And she'd send Kate a message in return.

Satisfied that she'd gathered everything she needed to rehearse at home, and anxious to get back to Parker, Kate turned to leave the room.

Her cell phone buzzed, scaring her with its shrill ringing. Thinking it might be her mother, Kate answered on the first ring. "Hello?"

"You have a very strange sense of humor."

Kate's heart vibrated hard against her rib cage. "Penny?"

"You want to know the truth? You want to end this?"

"Yes, yes, I do. Just talk to me. Help me to understand."

"Okay, I will. You think I left you all those things, don't you? Well, think again. Parker showed you the locket, right? Parker brought one of the sketches to you, right? And do you really know who left that locket at your house or that package at the hospital?"

Kate's body shook with rage. "How would *you* know about all of that if you weren't the one who did it?"

There was a long minute of silence, followed by a sigh. "Because I've been watching Parker, trying to get to the truth. And the truth is, he's the one setting you up, Kate. You're in a very dangerous situation, with a very dangerous man. And I can prove it." She named a place where Kate could meet her.

"How can I believe you?" Kate asked, wondering just how unstable Penny really was.

"Because of the real locket," the voice from the phone said. "Because the initials PB stand for more than just Parker's name. He killed Josie to hide the fact that he was her baby's father. He killed her, and she left that necklace with his initials on it to show he did it. If you don't believe me, just meet with me and I'll show you the real proof. But come alone. If you contact the police or bring anyone with you, I'll leave and it will only get worse for your dear Parker. And for his child."

"What are you saying?" Kate asked, her voice rising.

"I know where the child is."

Kate stood stunned as the connection was lost, those words echoing with an eerie clarity inside her head.

A child. There was a child out there somewhere that might belong to Parker.

She had no choice but to meet with Penny and find that child. And she had to do it now.

Parker's cell phone rang just as he turned to search for Kate. Still looking up and down the pews, he answered it, hoping it might be her.

"Parker, it's Jennifer. I'm worried about Kate."

Parker's heart hammered a warning. "She's here at church somewhere. What's wrong?"

"I was checking the Web site about an hour ago," Jennifer said, her voice shaky and breathless. "Kate put out a plea for information so she could clear your name. And we got a weird message, with a screen name of Daisy."

"Daisy?" Then Parker thought of the gaudy plastic

flower they'd found in Brandon's room. He hurried down the aisle and grabbed Nikki Rivers's sleeve, halting both the detectives at the back door of the church. "What did it say?"

"Something about a grand finale and wanting to bring about justice. It didn't make sense, but it sounded almost like a threat. I printed it out." She heaved a breath. "But the screen name caught my attention. Then I remembered Kate telling us about the weird clown at Brandon's party and how she'd found a flower in his room. I think it might have been Penny."

"Okay, thanks. I'm going to find Kate right now."

"Parker, there's something else. Kate and I did some research on tracking down Penny. Her last known address is in Charleston, but no one answers at that address. The phone has been disconnected. That could mean she's left for good, or it could mean she's here, just as we think. Kate kept talking about wanting to confront Penny. I've got a bad feeling about this."

"Let me find Kate." Parker clicked his phone shut, then turned to the detectives, using his cane to guide him. "Something's going on. We've got to find Kate." Dragging Nikki up the aisle, with Jim right on her heels, he quickly explained what Jennifer had told him. "Either Penny is after Kate, or Kate has gone out on her own to find Penny."

"That would be pretty dumb," Nikki said, but she'd already pulled out her notes to write down what Parker was telling her.

"Kate's not dumb," Parker retorted, wincing over his shoulder as they raced up toward the altar, "but she is tired of feeling unsafe, so I'm afraid she may have taken matters into her own hands."

And she has this crazy, impulsive streak, he wanted to add. Because she was so intent on protecting him, he thought, his heart pumping with adrenaline and shock as pain thrashed through his leg.

They called to some of the others who were leaving.

One of the choir members came running over, bobbing his head. "Yeah, I just saw her. She took off in your car, Parker."

Parker stopped, his breath heaving as he leaned on his cane to steady himself. "She's gone after her." Then he turned to the two detectives. "Now do you believe me! You've got to find her before Penny kills her."

Both Nikki and Jim rushed past Parker, but Nikki shouted over her shoulder, "Don't worry, we'll put out an APB on your car."

"I'm going with you," Parker shouted as he hurried to follow them.

Jim turned to push a hand against Parker's chest. "No, you will not. You'd just be in the way. Where's her son?"

"With her mother," Parker replied, a whole new set of worries surfacing.

"Go to the judge's house and wait there," Nikki said. "*Now,* Parker."

By this time, Reverend Rogers had heard most of the conversation. "I'll give you a ride, Parker."

Parker glanced up and down the street, then hit his cane against the asphalt. He'd never felt so helpless in his life. But since he didn't have a car, and since the officers were already speeding out of the parking lot, he had no choice but to go with Reverend Rogers. For now.

Once they were in the minister's car, he pulled out

his phone to call Kate. She didn't answer, so he left a message. "Just let me help you, Kate. Don't do this alone, please." Then he called Grace to check on Brandon. It took all his resolve to sound calm, but he didn't want to upset Grace until he had to.

Reverend Rogers made it to the Duncan home in record time. "I'll stay with y'all until we hear," he said, his expression grim.

Parker couldn't speak. He nodded, then got out of the car. How was he going to find the strength to get through this? Then he looked back at the minister. "I'm glad you're here, sir."

Reverend Rogers patted him on the back. "Let's go inside, son."

But something told Parker he couldn't do that. He couldn't just sit around, not knowing what kind of trap Kate might be walking into. "I need to borrow your car, Reverend," he said, his words solemn and firm.

"Son, I don't think—"

"I need to take your car," Parker said again, his voice rising. "Don't make me have to steal it."

Reverend Rogers nodded, then handed him the keys. "I won't make you do that, Parker. Just…be careful."

Parker turned toward the street. But he glanced back toward the minister. "Take care of Brandon for me, until I can bring his mother home."

"I will," the reverend said. "And I'll be in prayer for all of you."

Parker thought that was a very good idea. Somebody better pray for all of them, and especially for Penny Brighton.

SEVENTEEN

Kate pulled the car up to the seedy motel north of town, then circled around to the back where overgrown bushes and a couple of junked cars obscured most of the rooms. Parker's slick black sports car stood out in this beat-up parking lot like a diamond in a pile of coal, but she hoped that would work to her advantage. Parker would have missed her by now, and he'd know something wasn't right. He'd alert the police as soon as he realized his car was gone.

But she prayed he'd stay away from here. She didn't want anything to happen to him. Maybe if she could just talk to Penny, she could get to the bottom of all the mystery surrounding Josie's death and finally clear Parker.

A steady stream of prayers moving through her head, she got out of the car and carefully walked to the bottom-floor room where Penny had told her she'd be waiting. Heaving a sigh, Kate reached up to knock. But before she could, the door swung open.

And she stood face-to-face with Penny Brighton.

Penny hadn't aged gracefully. Her dark-blond hair had a dirty sheen to it and her skin looked pinched and pressed, the pallor a sickly white, probably from lack of sleep. She was wearing all black—a black dirty T-shirt and matching black jeans and sandals. Which made sense, Kate couldn't help thinking, since she obviously lurked about at night stalking people.

"Hello, Kate," Penny said, her smile bright, her eyes shining.

Too bright and too shining, Kate decided. The woman looked mentally unstable. "Hello, Penny. Let's just get this over with."

Penny motioned Kate in, then glanced around the quiet, deserted parking lot. "No one followed you, right?"

Kate dropped her tote bag on a chair. "No." The less she said, the better.

"Good, then." Penny shut the door then twirled to stare at Kate. "You haven't changed much."

"Apparently, neither have you," Kate retorted, taking inventory of the shabby room. Penny's messy nature seemed as she remembered it. Clothes and shoes were strewn all around the small room. The efficiency kitchen lining one wall was covered with take-out boxes and soda cans. And the long dresser was layered with various scarves and wigs. "Been holed up here for a while, have you?"

Penny shrugged. "You could say that. I had to come back to prove that Parker is a murderer."

Kate rounded on her. "No, Penny, you had to come back to cover the fact that you somehow murdered your best friend. You did kill Josie, didn't you?"

Penny looked startled, but placed her hands together and stood tall. "You have no idea what I've been through over the last ten years."

"No, I don't. So why don't you tell me?" Kate said, getting close so Penny would see the intent in her eyes. "Because before I leave here, I'm going to get some answers. One way or another."

"Oh, I plan to give you answers," Penny said, her eyes going eerily bright again. "One way or another." Then she came at Kate, and everything went black.

Parker had a hard time adjusting to the minister's car, but in spite of straining his hurting leg to push at the gas pedal and brakes, he managed to drive the car without breaking any laws. Trying to drive the unfamiliar car while searching the town wasn't easy. "Kate, where are you?" he said, hitting a hand against the steering wheel.

Think, he told himself. *If you were hiding out in a town where everyone knew you, where would you go? Where would you hide?*

He thought about Penny and what was motivating her. Obviously, she was trying to cover up something. Either she'd killed Josie, or she knew who had. She'd probably been the one behind *all* the odd happenings around here. She might even have been involved in Scott Winters's murder. Then there were the anonymous tips to the police, the vandalisms and the stalkings. But why would she target all of her classmates, especially Kate?

She hates me, Parker thought, *because of the wreck.*

But he had been the one to suffer the most from that wreck. Penny had received only minor injuries, nothing lasting or damaging. Or...had she suffered more than anyone knew? Was there some reason the wreck could have caused her to want to lash out at all her classmates?

The Kesslers had shunned her after Adam's death, because they believed her child wasn't Adam's. And, he remembered—a cold chill sweeping over his body— Kate had told him that the Kesslers didn't believe Adam's death had been an accident. Could Penny have been involved in that, too? She'd have it in for Steff for that reason alone, he supposed. She'd targeted the alumni Web site because the group was searching for answers. But what was Penny trying so desperately to hide? Surely she couldn't have been involved in three different murders?

If he didn't find Kate soon, that number might become four.

He moved up and down the streets past the college. Would she have taken Kate back to the scene of the crime?

That would be too obvious. But Penny wasn't thinking clearly.

He trolled the parking lots of the vast campus. The sun was setting and soon it would be hard to see anything but shadows and trees. Finally, he stopped the car and laid his head against the steering wheel. "I need Your help, Lord. I need to find Kate. I know I haven't been faithful, so I won't bargain or plead for my sake. But don't let Kate come to harm. Please, for Brandon's sake. And because...I need them both in my life. Help me, Lord. Help me."

Parker sat for a while, quiet and still, his heart beating like a gentle drum inside his body. Then a thought came to his mind. What would Patchman do in this situation?

He almost laughed out loud. Here he was, alone and helpless, trying to save the woman he loved, and he was relying on his own comic-book superhero to help him.

No, he was asking a very real, living God to help him. And he could see it so clearly in his mind now. Patchman had always represented the principles of Christ. Parker had never planned it that way; had never set out to teach anyone moral lessons. But it was all right there in his art and in his stories. Truth and honor and faith shined in all of his comic-book hero's deeds.

"Help me, Lord," he said out into the night.

Then a memory swirled inside his mind, as clear and precise as if he were drawing the scene. He saw Patchman racing to save a friend. A friend was trapped in an old hotel. Parker closed his eyes, picturing the blinking lights of the neon sign coming through the hotel's window.

That scene had been in one of his earlier strips.

But the more he thought about it, the more it made sense. Wouldn't Penny prefer hiding out in some shabby hotel or apartment building rather than staying near the more upscale, historical buildings around the campus?

What would he do if he were trying to hide in plain sight?

Parker cranked the car and hurried to the outskirts of town.

Penny laughed as she stared down at Kate, her grip tightening against the rope she'd tied around Kate's hands. Kate was coming to quickly, though she seemed confused and disoriented. Coming around from behind the chair, Penny leaned close. "Here's the plan. You're going to die tonight, in much the same way Josie died ten years ago. And Parker is going to be the one arrested for your murder. You see, he got close to you in order to win you over, but in truth, he only wanted you near so he could watch you and plan how to keep you and your nosy little church friends from finding out the truth. He killed Josie and now he's going to kill you. Then the truth will be out at last. Parker will go to jail, and my work here will be done."

Kate sat listening, stunned and shocked by the dangerous gleam in Penny's eyes. "But why do you want to do this to Parker? What did he do to you, Penny? What have any of us done to you?"

Penny groaned low in her throat. "*He* did this to Josie. He killed her. He's responsible. Just as responsible as I am. And you all deserve to pay. Parker especially. He killed Josie and he killed *my* baby."

Kate hitched a breath. "What are you saying? *Your* child is safe, right? But where is Josie's child?"

Ignoring her, Penny started grabbing things, tossing them inside a big bag. Keys, maps, bottles, ropes. Kate didn't want to know what she was packing. She didn't plan on dying tonight.

Straining against the ropes holding her hands behind her chair, she said, "Look, Penny, you said you have proof that Parker killed Josie. You said you know where Josie's child is. Tell me the truth. If you'll just talk to me, we can help you."

Then Penny whirled around, a gun pointed at Kate. "You want to hear the truth? I'll tell you. But first, we have to get out of here." Then she turned back to her work. "Now don't make me have to use this gun too soon, Kate. Just sit tight until I have everything we need."

Kate glanced around, searching for a way to end this.

She couldn't leave this room with Penny Brighton. She knew if she did, she'd never see Parker or her son again.

Watching as Penny frantically gathered things, Kate scanned the musty, humid room. Then she glanced behind her to the night table right by her narrow chair and saw the clown mask Penny must have used to get inside the birthday party. And lying beside that was a brochure featuring historical sites around Magnolia Falls. One of those sites was Magnolia Hall. Parker's house.

Kate knew what she had to do. It would be the only way to leave Parker a clue. Looking up to make sure Penny couldn't see, she leaned back, straining against the chair, wincing as her arms stretched to a painful tear. But she managed to wiggle her fingers enough to push the clown mask down to the floor. Then with a slow-motion effort, using her bound hands, she flicked the brochure off the table, watching as it landed near the mask. Now all she had to do was get her stretch-band watch off her wrist and drop that down beside the brochure.

Dear God, please let Parker or the police see this. Please let them find me.

Parker had checked every low-budget hotel and motel out on the interstate and along the incoming highways to the town. Feeling hopeless, he tried to call Nikki Rivers at the police station, but he was put on hold and finally gave up. Nikki should be out looking, too, he hoped.

One last motel came to mind. It was a rough little place off the beaten path in a bad part of town. Parker only thought about it because he'd grown up not far from it. He doubted someone as self-centered and crazy as Penny would want to stay there. But it was worth a shot.

He rounded a corner and saw the flashing neon sign advertising the motel—the Daisy Blossom. This was about the only place in town that didn't have the word *magnolia* in its name.

Daisy.

His dog was named Daisy.

The screen name Jennifer had spotted was Daisy.

And now, here he was at the Daisy Blossom Motel.

And the big neon flower on the sign was flashing a bright yellow and white.

Parker's whole system went on full alert as he gunned the engine and sped into the parking lot.

Kate drove Parker's car very slowly, hoping someone would spot them and pull them over. But she couldn't stop. Penny had a gun pointed toward her ribs.

"Where are we going?" she asked. She'd tried to get Penny talking, but the other woman, disguised in a short black wig and dark shades, seemed intent on staying on the winding back roads. It was now fully dark and since Kate wasn't familiar with these roads or the specially-built, handicapped driving mechanisms of the car, she had to concentrate on her driving.

Finally, Penny pointed to the right. "Turn here."

Kate slid the sleek car onto a gravel lane. "Where are we going, Penny? You can at least tell me that."

"You'll know soon enough," Penny said, a soft chuckle gurgling in her throat.

Kate watched the road as they rounded a curve, then gasped. "Parker's house?"

"Exactly," Penny said, grinning. "I found a back way in. Parker doesn't have a high-tech security gate way back here. It was easy to cut the lock on the old wooden gate."

Kate couldn't fathom how much hate Penny seemed consumed by. But now that she knew where she was, at least she could get a handle on how to get away from Penny. If she was correct, the pond would be straight ahead and the house just up the hill from that. She'd just have to make a run for it.

But they didn't stop at the pond. Penny instructed her to go past it and up the rut-filled lane to the yard. "Park here," she instructed. "Don't move until I come around the car."

Kate did as Penny told her, glancing around and waiting for her chance to get away. She had no idea why Penny had brought her here, but then she didn't think even Penny understood that. Penny Brighton was too far gone to be reasonable. And that made her very dangerous.

But that also gave Kate an advantage. Because in spite of being terrified, she was still rational. She knew how to be strong when things seemed at their most dire.

After circling the parking lot twice and not seeing his car, Parker rushed to the front desk of the motel, startling the dozing clerk. "I need your help. It's an emergency. I'm looking for a woman. Blond maybe. Petite. She would have been renting a room on and off for a few months now. Comes and goes."

The chubby clerk looked at him as if he'd gone completely daft. "You just described half of our clientele."

Parker ran a hand over his hair in frustration. "But can you think of anyone who's been here on a long-term basis? She'd pay in cash. And she wouldn't be very friendly or forthcoming."

The clerk rubbed his beard stubble. "Well, now, there is that pretty little thing that works part-time as some sort of actress. Always wearing a different costume. Even works as a clown here and there, from what I've seen." He leaned forward. "And she ain't friendly at all, let me tell you."

"I need to see her room," Parker said, pulling out his wallet. "And I'm willing to pay you whatever it takes."

The clerk's beady eyes lit up. "Well, that's the best offer I've had all night."

Parker followed the man around the corner and waited as the clerk knocked. Frustrated, he said, "She's not in there. Open the door."

"Okay, all right, hold your horses."

Parker's cell phone rang. "Kate?"

"No, it's Nikki. Where are you?"

"I'm out looking for Kate."

"We told you to sit tight."

"I can't do that. Tell me you've found them."

"No, not yet. And we can't locate your car, either. We're searching, Parker. We've got patrols everywhere."

"Well, keep searching," Parker said. Then he told Nikki where he was. "I'm about to go into the room we think is Penny's."

"I'm not even going to ask how you managed that particular stunt," Nikki said.

"Good," Parker retorted. Then he hung up.

And looked into a room that represented all of his worst nightmares.

"Your friend ain't here," the desk clerk pointed out. "Sure is a messy little thing."

Parker scanned the room, hoping for some sign from Kate. Then he saw something familiar. A clown's mask with bright yellow hair lying beside an overturned chair. Rushing past the confused clerk, Parker grabbed up the garish mask. He'd seen this very mask at Brandon's party. Throwing it down, he turned to leave, but his foot brushed against a piece of paper.

He picked it up. It was a brochure featuring Magnolia Hall. He remembered the Chamber of Commerce calling him to get permission to feature his home on the front of the brochure. No tours, they'd said, just the historical significance of the big house.

Penny had been very thorough in researching his house. His eye caught something else lying there by the chair. Something shiny and gold. He reached to pick it up. It was Kate's watch.

"Look, I don't have all night and I could get in serious trouble if she comes back and finds us in here."

Parker turned to stare at the clerk. "That's okay. I'm done."

He whirled toward the door, his cane almost knocking the man down. "Tell the police to come to Magnolia Hall," he called over his shoulder. "Tell them to hurry."

"You're welcome," the clerk called.

Parker heard the sirens blasting toward the motel, but

he was peeling out of the driveway before the police ever made it into the parking lot. The desk clerk could explain things to the detectives.

He was headed toward home.

They walked up to the pool. Kate could hear the dogs barking inside the house.

Penny pushed her toward the sparkling water. "We have to hurry. Parker has so many cameras around here, I'm sure we'll trip some sort of alarm. But I'll be long gone before anyone comes for you." Then she turned Kate around. "And you'll be floating in the pool by then."

Kate stared at the woman standing in front of her. "You killed Josie, didn't you?"

Penny nodded, a soft smile on her face. "I didn't want to. But I had no choice." Then she sighed. "It's almost a relief, finally being able to admit that. But you won't tell, will you, Kate? No one will ever know. And Parker will be blamed. I've set it all up. I just have one final piece of evidence to leave for the cops."

She pulled something out of her shoulder bag, then handed it to Kate. "Look at her—that's Parker's daughter."

Kate took the small picture, staring at it in the muted security light. The dark-haired little girl looked to be around nine or ten. Turning slightly, she held it up to the light. "What's her name?"

"Alexis," Penny said, smiling.

"But that's your daughter's name, isn't it?"

"That's right," Penny said, her tone hushed. "Give it back. I wanted you to see her before you die. I'll leave this somewhere the police are sure to find it. And then, this will finally be over." She giggled. "I've left a strand of Parker's hair tucked into that picture frame. That should be proof enough that he killed you and that he knows about this child."

Kate took one last look at the pretty little girl in the picture. Then she let out a gasp of shock. "This…this little girl looks just like Josie."

"Give it to me," Penny shouted, waving the gun in Kate's face. "It's time to end this."

"Oh, no," Kate said, her hand flying to her mouth. "You killed Josie and took her child, didn't you?"

"You don't understand anything," Penny said, her shouts shrill. "You don't know what I've been through."

"I don't believe that," Kate said, backing away even as Penny aimed the gun at her.

"The wreck killed my baby. And after that, I couldn't have any more. It ruined everything—Adam hated me and his family didn't want me around. I lost the only man I ever loved. So I left with Josie."

"This isn't your daughter."

"She's my daughter in every way that counts," Penny screamed. "And she's safe. You'll never find her. Parker will never see her. And her real father won't either."

Kate could tell Penny was falling apart. "Her *real* father? Who's her real father, Penny? Tell me before you kill me. You owe me that, at least."

Penny looked confused, her gaze darting here and there. "I told you, it's Parker. Now give me the picture."

Kate couldn't let it go. If she died, she could at least die knowing the truth. "Penny, let me help you. We can all help you."

But Penny was done listening. Knocking the picture to the ground, she advanced on Kate, the gun held high. "I'm sorry, Kate. Really I am."

Kate braced herself. Her only chance was to dive into the pool and hope Penny would miss. But just as she readied herself for the worst, she heard someone shouting her name.

"Kate!"

And then she heard the dogs barking and snarling. Parker must have let them out.

Penny heard them, too, and panicked. Whirling, she shot toward the dogs, too high, then frantically turned the gun toward Kate. Kate saw Penny's arm lifting, heard the dogs approaching, then watched in amazement as something sleek and solid whacked through the air toward Penny's uplifted arm. Parker's silver-tipped cane! Penny screamed just as the gun fired.

A searing pain pulsed in Kate's arm as she slipped and toppled, the cool waters of the pool surrounding her. She'd been shot. That was her last thought as her world went black for the second time that night.

Parker saw Kate fall into the pool and, his heart pumping, dived in after her. Slicing through the water, he grabbed Kate by the waist and pulled her to the surface, using all of his energy to tug her onto the steps.

"Kate, Kate, honey, stay with me," he said, noting the deathly pallor of her skin. "Kate?"

He heard the sirens on the road. He heard the dogs barking toward the back of the yard. And he had no idea where Penny had gone. But he had to help Kate.

Carefully, he lifted her out of the water and onto the

deck, then began giving her CPR. After a few puffs and a lot of prayer, she finally moaned, then spat out water. "Parker?"

"I'm here, right here." He breathed a heavy sigh, then held her in his arms. "I'm here. It's over."

"She's gone," Nikki told him about an hour later. "We think she must have run into the pool house, since the dogs keep whining and sniffing around the door. "But she's not in there now and your car is gone. Probably ran through the woods when you were getting Kate out of the pool."

"Can't you find her?" Parker asked, his hand holding tightly to Kate's.

"We'll keep trying," Nikki said, a promise in her eyes. "She's clever and she's scared. Most likely, we'll find your car abandoned somewhere. As for Penny Brighton…well, she's got a lot of explaining to do."

Kate took a sip of the hot tea Parker had insisted she drink after nearly drowning. The paramedics had examined her arm and declared it a flesh wound, which she had assured Parker it was anyway. Now the entire house was swarming with police officers and crime scene investigators.

"I'm so tired," she told Parker. "I just want to see Brandon."

"Your mother says he's fine, but I'll take you home in a little while," he told her, kissing the top of her damp hair. Then he pulled the blanket closer around her. "Just rest."

Nikki looked down at them where they sat in the big den. "Kate, I know this has been rough. But if what you told us is true, then you've helped solve a major crime."

Then she turned as Jim Anderson walked over to them. "What's the latest?"

Jim looked grim. "The good news—Cornell Rutherford just copped a plea, based on the fact that Penny Brighton tried to kill Kate tonight. He's willing to spill his guts. No telling what we'll find out from that."

Parker pulled Kate close. "I think you'll find out Penny killed Josie and probably Adam Kessler, too."

"And possibly Scott Winters," Kate added. Then she glanced up at Nikki. "We need to warn Jennifer."

"Why's that?"

"So far, Penny has gone after everyone involved in the Web site. She has to know Jennifer is helping out. And Jennifer's the only one left. The only one Penny hasn't targeted."

"I'll get right on that," Nikki said.

After another hour of questions, the police finally left and the house was quiet. It was just the two of them and the dogs.

Kate snuggled close, the security of being in Parker's arms warming her heart. "I love you," she said. She felt the flutter of his heartbeat.

"I love you. I have always loved you." He tugged her head up, then kissed her. "And you always believed in me."

"Yes, I believed in you."

"Did I ever tell you about the night of the wreck?"

"No, not much."

"I was coming to see you," he explained. "I wanted to ask you out on a date."

She smiled. Kissed him again. "So it only took you ten years?"

"More or less."

He wrapped his arms around her. "You're safe now, Kate."

"I know."

She looked out into the dark night, savoring the feeling of being safe and loved. And she prayed Jennifer would be safe, too. After all, they'd had enough death and pain because of Penny's warped mind. More than enough.

Somewhere north of the city, a lone figure dressed in dark clothing walked in and out of the shadows of the great moss-covered live oaks. Finally, tired and frustrated, the woman sank down beside the flowing river, sobbing and gasping as she realized she'd failed one more time.

Penny Brighton hadn't managed to frame Parker after all. She hadn't managed to hurt any of the people who'd discovered her hidden secret buried on the campus of Magnolia Falls College.

But she dried her eyes and held her head up.

That only left one last chance. There had to be a way to end all of this.

She got up, wiped off her clothes and started heading toward the lights of the interstate. She'd have to hide out and think things through. But she still had one important piece of evidence that no one would be able to find. She still had Josie's child. She still had Alexis.

* * * * *

In June 2008, don't miss the thrilling conclusion to
REUNION REVELATIONS, FINAL JUSTICE
by Marta Perry.

Dear Reader,

I enjoyed working with the other writers on this continuity. It was a challenge because none of us had ever done anything with such an intense plot that involved a decade-old murder! But we put our heads together and worked out the details with compromise and with a lot of imagination.

God puts certain people in our lives at just the right time to help us through the tough spots. We might not realize that, but His hand is in every step we take. This is the lesson Parker and Kate had to learn in my story. I loved these characters, who had been so close in college. I'm glad they were able to find each other again at just the right time. Parker was an interesting character and I had fun with his different quirks. While this story was challenging, it taught me a lot about trusting in others and working with a good team. Many thanks to everyone involved. I hope you enjoy the whole series.

And I hope that this story might encourage you to have a reunion with someone you've missed. Through faith and trust, we can find old friends again. And we can find God again. He is always there, in shadows and in the light.

Until next time, may the angels watch over you always.

Lenora Worth

QUESTIONS FOR DISCUSSION

1. This is a story about secrets and past hurts. Do you have things in your past that you can't seem to let go of? How do you cope with them?

2. Why did Parker return to Magnolia Falls? What feelings do you think he had about returning to the town?

3. Why did Kate avoid Parker for so long? Is there someone from your past that you avoided? What was it like when you saw them again?

4. Kate went through a horrible divorce. Do you think she did the right thing in getting a divorce? Do you think marriage is forever or are there some instances where divorce is warranted? Discuss.

5. Kate and her friends have become close again since college. Do you have good friends in whom you put a lot of trust? Do you keep in touch with old school friends? How do you think old friendships differ from newer friendships?

6. Parker's accident left him bitter and angry. Do you have things in your past that have separated you from God's love? How did you overcome them? If you haven't been through this yourself, discuss the experience of someone you know.

7. Kate was a bit impulsive at times. How did she learn to control her impulsive nature? Do you think Parker helped her to be calmer?

8. Kate loved her son and wanted to protect him above everything else. She took a risk in going to Parker's house. Do you think that was wise? What would you have done in her situation?

9. How did Kate's faith in God help her through all the danger she felt around her? Have you ever turned to God in times of fear? Describe such an instance.

10. What helped Parker finally find where Penny had taken Kate? Do you believe God shows us things in life to help us? Give an example from your life.

11. Why did Kate's mother try so hard at first to keep her away from Parker? How did Parker finally win her over?

12. Why was Penny so intent on making everyone else suffer for all her troubles? Why did she feel justified in ruining Parker? Do you think Penny felt abandoned and alone? How could God's love have helped her overcome all her problems?

13. How did finding Kate again help Parker return to God? Do you know other people who have come to God through the help of a loved one? Discuss an

instance when you helped someone strengthen his or her faith. How has someone you love helped you with your faith?

REQUEST YOUR FREE BOOKS!

2 FREE RIVETING INSPIRATIONAL NOVELS
PLUS 2 FREE MYSTERY GIFTS

Love Inspired SUSPENSE

YES! Please send me 2 FREE Love Inspired® Suspense novels and my 2 FREE mystery gifts (gifts are worth about $10). After receiving them, if I don't wish to receive any more books, I can return the shipping statement marked "cancel". If I don't cancel, I will receive 4 brand-new novels every month and be billed just $4.24 per book in the U.S. or $4.74 per book in Canada, plus 25¢ shipping and handling per book and applicable taxes, if any*. That's a savings of over 20% off the cover price! I understand that accepting the 2 free books and gifts places me under no obligation to buy anything. I can always return a shipment and cancel at any time. Even if I never buy another book, the two free books and gifts are mine to keep forever.

123 IDN ERXX   323 IDN ERXM

Name	(PLEASE PRINT)
Address	Apt. #
City	State/Prov.	Zip/Postal Code

Signature (if under 18, a parent or guardian must sign)

Order online at www.LoveInspiredSuspense.com

Or mail to Steeple Hill Reader Service:

IN U.S.A.: P.O. Box 1867, Buffalo, NY 14240-1867
IN CANADA: P.O. Box 609, Fort Erie, Ontario L2A 5X3

Not valid to current subscribers of Love Inspired Suspense books.

Want to try two free books from another series?
Call 1-800-873-8635 or visit www.morefreebooks.com

* Terms and prices subject to change without notice. N.Y. residents add applicable sales tax. Canadian residents will be charged applicable provincial taxes and GST. This offer is limited to one order per household. All orders subject to approval. Credit or debit balances in a customer's account(s) may be offset by any other outstanding balance owed by or to the customer. Please allow 4 to 6 weeks for delivery. Offer available while quantities last.

Your Privacy: Steeple Hill Books is committed to protecting your privacy. Our Privacy Policy is available online at www.SteepleHill.com or upon request from the Reader Service. From time to time we make our lists of customers available to reputable third parties who may have a product or service of interest to you. If you would prefer we not share your name and address, please check here. ☐

LISUS08

Love Inspired®
SUSPENSE

TITLES AVAILABLE NEXT MONTH

Don't miss these four stories in June

BAYOU PARADOX by Robin Caroll

When a mysterious illness strikes down two women in Tara LeBlanc's life, she knows she's the one who will find the cause. By-the-book sheriff Bubba Theriot has his hands full trying to track down the suspects *and* keep Tara safe from the bayou, the culprits and her own dangerous instincts.

FINAL JUSTICE by Marta Perry
Reunion Revelations

The DNA test proves it: Mason Grant is a father. What's more, his nine-year-old daughter has been in the custody of her mother's killer all these years. With the help of old college friend Jennifer Pappas, Mason tries to adjust to fatherhood, but the killer isn't through with them yet.

KEEPING HER SAFE by Barbara Phinney

Hunter Gordon would have done anything for the Bentons—he'd even plead guilty to a crime he hadn't committed. Now that Rae Benton is in danger, Hunter is determined to keep her safe...if Rae will let him. But before he can help her, Hunter will have to win back her trust.

KILLER CARGO by Dana Mentink

Pilot Maria de Silva is shocked to find a hidden stash of drugs in the midst of the pet supplies she's delivering. Her only refuge in an unfamiliar town is Cy Sheridan's animal sanctuary. Can Cy protect her from the danger that lurks outside?

LISCNM0508